RANDOM BIRTHS
AND
LOVE HEARTS

RANDOM BIRTHS
AND
LOVE HEARTS

Catrin Dafydd

Gomer

Published in 2015 by
Gomer Press, Llandysul, Ceredigion, SA44 4JL

ISBN 978 1 84851 737 0
ISBN 978 1 78562 011 9 (ePUB)
ISBN 978 1 78562 012 6 (Kindle)

A CIP record for this title is available from the British Library.
© Copyright Catrin Dafydd 2015

P. 56 'Pwy wnaeth y sêr uwchben?'
© Cyhoeddiadau Curiad
Words and music: Arfon Wyn
Reproduced by kind permission of the publisher

Thank you to Magdalen Maguire, who made a donation
to Autistica to have her name included as a character.

Catrin Dafydd asserts her moral right under the
Copyright, Designs and Patents Act 1988
to be identified as the author of this work.

This book is published with the financial support of the
Welsh Books Council.

Printed and bound in Wales at
Gomer Press, Llandysul, Ceredigion
www.gomer.co.uk

You're mine

'Mam! I am NOT goin' to any Ann Summers party. Just stop hasslin' me about it.'

'Oh come on mun, love, loosen up a bit, will ew? Only a couple of us it'll be!'

I frown at her, stop the trolley from movin'. I do love her, obviously. I mean, she's my Mam, but she sometimes thinks she knows best, when she really doesn't. She's shorter than me, too, I realise as I look at her. Funny that, how you can come out of someone and then be taller than them in the long run.

I speak in hushed tones, don't want little Gwen to hear us. 'Mam. Listen, right. I'm NOT goin' round in circles like this again. Havin' a vibrator flung in my face is not my idea of bein' cheered up.'

'Who's tryin' to cheer you up?' she asks, all doe-eyed as she smiles down at little Gwen, whose blond hair is slowly wrapping itself around the shiny metal bars of the trolley.

With a gulp of breath, Gwen remembers something she must tell us immediately: 'Miss Llewelyn said I was the bestest at Lluniau Lliw today. Better than Calypso and Rhian.'

'There's good,' I say, before I turn back to Mam. 'You don't need to worry about me, I'm right as rain.' But Mam looks at me at that moment and nearly breaks my heart. She knows me well enough to know that when I say things like that I'm blatantly struggling. Her eyes are screaming the sentence, Richard is a bastard. Richard is a selfish little bastard.

'Just cancel it, yeah?' I ask her, my eyes as wide as I can make them. Only she obviously has other ideas.

'A bit o' fun, a bit o' wine, that's all I was thinking. But there we are.' She's silent for a moment. Staging a protest. And then, just like that, she's off again. 'Be nice round your flat, mind. Could pull the sofa back, ask Arse to come over …' She pushes the trolley again. 'Let's get those frozen burger thingies, isit?'

Gwen grabs hold of a packet of Wagon Wheels, eyeballs me.

'Nope, sorry,' I say, turning away from her, only because I know I've only just got enough for toilet paper in my purse, let alone some shit we really don't need.

Little Gwen looks appalled. 'But Bampy Terry lets me,' and I watch her dragging her little shoes behind her, hangin' on the trolley like a bloody monkey. I swear she thinks the sun shines out of that-man-Terry's arse. Bampy Terry this. Bampy Terry that. Bampy Terry sings Queen to me on the way to school. Bampy Terry told this joke. It's enough to drive you bananas.

'Mam do you tea when we get back now,' I say, and little Gwen sulks with her shoulders. She looks so pretty this afternoon. All perfect in her scruffy-lookin' uniform. I was never blonde like her, apparently. Always a little bit freckly, always light brown. But pretty eyes. Pretty,

pretty eyes I've always had. Least that's what Nanna used to say. Sayin' that, she was half-blind by the time I came out. But I think I know what she meant. They can charm people, my eyes.

As Mam pushes the trolley, I notice how tired she's lookin'. Granted, she's just come straight from work, but fair play, she's lookin' awful. Her hair's flat, her nose's red and her make-up's all smudgy. Bein' a nurse ain't no joke, I think to myself as I peer at the deep wrinkles that have established themselves on her face. Due to her smilin' and bein' kind to everyone, that is. Wrinkles for bein' nice.

'Who's Ann Summer?' little Gwen asks with innocence flowing from her like some cold wind.

'A lady who's not comin' round our house,' I say, and I smile at Mam.

Lookin' at her, I can tell she's not goin' to give up. Hellish powerful mind she's got. Steamrolls over everythin'.

'I want tŷ bach, Mam,' and as Gwen says this, Mam looks at me with a strange emotion in her eyes.

'God. Seems like only yesterday you used to say tŷ bach. I wonder where it all goes when you grow up.'

'I'm burstin'…' and the threat of it is enough to drive me nuts. So I rush to the checkout, put some things on the conveyor belt, watch my daughter doubled up, trying not to let anything slip out.

Mam loads a few other things onto the smelly conveyor belt and I notice a few items that Gwen has managed to sneak through. Mam clocks me looking at them and she stuffs some money in my hand.

'I'll get this shop.' I look at her. Annoyed at the fact that I'm not going to be able to refuse. Chuffed and annoyed at the same time. 'Pay me back when you get your next pay from the caff.'

Gwen has plonked herself on the window-ledge by now, next to a tower of cardboard boxes. She smiles at me, my little daughter. Crosses her legs and holds her hands tight over her belly. She's burstin' but still happy to give me a smile. That's my girl. As I watch the woman in front of us paying for her things, I start thinking about wee, and the idea of drinkin' water. And it goin' through you. Through all your tubes. And that it has to come out. The other end. Weird, it can be sometimes, to actually think about crazy things like that. The fact that you have to drink water to stay alive. The fact that this stuff is constantly running through you like a stream. We're just like pot plants really, I think to myself, before I grab the plastic bags I've brought with me to spare ten pence.

I'm just about to start packing the items when my phone vibrates. I pause for a moment and check it. It's a text from Arse.

Lookin frwd 2 the Ann Summers thing! Ewer Mam's a leg x

I look up at Mam, who's already busy packing. She's got a skull full of silly ideas, and she's confident enough to think she should put them into action. And the most annoying thing is I know I've already lost the battle with this Ann Summers thing. It's happenin'. End of. As I start packing, I spot a packet of Love Hearts amongst the burgers and the two-for-one frozen chips.

I pick the packet up, and look at it. Bloody Love Hearts. At this very moment in time, they seem to represent everythin' I hate about life. All the lies and the bollocks you're supposed to believe. All the shit dreams about love and sex.

'Can I leave these on the side?' I ask the young man behind the counter. Looking at him, I clock that he's actually very good looking. Blue eyes like the water on a tropical beach. Full lips that, fortunately for him, have always just been a lovely shape. For a moment, I imagine myself kissing him. Both of us against the wall of the supermarket. His hand on my thigh. Then I snap back to reality. Realise he's probably just as unreliable as the rest of them.

I'm annoyed with myself for allowing such a stupid funny feelin'. That funny feelin' that leads you nowhere. It's the same dream that's peddled every time you open those Love Hearts. Like as if each and every message means something. Leads you closer to that one person you were always destined to meet. In a strange moment of nostalgia, I grab the packet and decide to buy them anyway. It's not that I want them, it's just that they've reminded me of someone I used to be. Before life got hold of me. Before I got to see that it was all just adverts, telling me how it could be. I buy them for the teenager I was. The sheer naivety of it takes my breath away.

I watch Mam packing for a moment. Methodically. Quietly. Then I look up at my daughter. Me and her against the world and Richard nowhere to be seen. Defeated, I reach into my pocket for the money Mam's just given me. Hand it over to the boy with the eyes. He doesn't even look up at me. Just takes it, and files it away in the till. It seems his eyes are nicer than the personality behind them, I think to myself. And that should never be the case.

You're gorgeous

It's all goin' off in my flat tonight.

Arse is here, left the kids at home with Alan. And Mam's here too. With bells on. And the woman from Lovelife.com, how could I have forgotten her. Mam found this cheaper local company in the end. Instead of Ann Summers. Lovelife.com. Cheap at half the price and a friend of a friend.

We've had the first part of the session. And now we're having a five-minute break before we begin part two. While I get the chance, I down a glass of water before I get forced to drink the best part of a bottle of wine to relax. Molly is lying under the kitchen table. She's so patient, that dog. She must be so heavy with those pups by now, but she seems to just lie there, and accept that it's all to come. I swear, we could all learn a lot from that dog.

'Don't make me go back for round two,' I say, looking at Arse with desperate eyes. She laughs, and makes me envious with the look of her. Best friends since school, and I still hate her for how she looks. Tiny and compact. Curvy in all the right places. Driving all the boys mad from the moment she landed on this earth.

'Don't be stupid, mun!' her little-mouse voice breaks through the air like vinegar through cream. 'We're doin' the toys next. And 'sides, it's all good fun!' and she wiggles her tight bum without even knowing she's done it.

'Tell her I've had to go lie down, will you? Got a temperature.'

Arse throws me over a look just as Mary pops back into the kitchen with her annoyin' smile. I mean, Mary. Shouldn't be bloody legal, to have such a religious name and do such a dirty job. Without meanin' to, I look her up and down and notice that she's over-sized in a really weird kind of way. It's not that she's fat, but she's got big features and tiny features. Little drainpipe legs and a big middle. Small shoulders and a heavy-lookin' head with plenty of frizzy blond hair. Big eyes she've got too. Big eyes like poppy-out boiled eggs.

'Girlies! When ewer ready …!' and I watch her pink top dancing around my little flat. Her muffin-top is something to be marvelled at. She darts back into the lounge and I hear her and Mam laughing their heads off.

'Girlies!' I hear Mary's fake chant again and Arse pulls me by the hand with an understanding glance.

'Very modern name, isn't it?' I can hear my Mam saying to Mary. Mary's bright colours are effing and blinding at everything else in the room. She's swearing with colour. She's put enough eyeshadow on her lids to last a year.

'Aye, well, me and Clio were out one night, and we were tryin' to think of names, you know. And it's obviously catched on, 'cos, bloomin' 'eck, we've got at least twenty girls workin' for us now.'

Clio can only be a car, I'm thinkin' to myself. Arse isn't really concentrating. She's leaning over to her handbag to check her phone. Her county-councillor husband, Alan, is looking after the children, and she can't trust him to close the front door properly, let alone work the oven and feed the kids.

'How do you get your bookings, then? Through the website, is it?' I ask, even though I don't really care.

'Haven't got a website,' Mary says, dull as hell.

'But you're called Lovelife.COM,' I say, gulping back some of the white wine. It's sharp on my tongue as I watch her wangle her way through the answer.

'Everyone puts a dot com after everythin' now, see love. Sounds cool. That's why we done it,' and she smiles, trying to draw attention to this product she has in her hand. I'm in a funny mood now. I'm sort of determined to catch her out about everything. I know she's on commission for every damn item she's got in that bag. And she's charged us thirty pound a head already anyway.

Arse pops her eyes back into our world.

'Kids okay?' My question oozes with friendliness.

'Aye,' she says. For some reason, in that moment, I notice that she looks older around the eyes. I reckon something's worrying her deep back somewhere. I don't know what, but there is something.

'Right then, girlies! If you wouldn't mind switchin' the music I brought back on …' I reach over to her little CD player and press play. All the songs from all the 80s films you can ever imagine have been chosen to woo us into feelin' horny and buyin' sex toys.

I gargle on my wine like a kid and Mam just looks at me funny.

'Okay!' Mary is preparing herself for her next performance. She did creams and kinky clothes before the break, but I can feel it in my bones what's coming next. Lookin' at her at that moment, I kind of feel for her. Wonder whether she's a Mam too.

'Now, I've got a really *beautiful* product for you next. Gorgeous it is. Just the thing for you gorgeous women! As you can see, this is …'

'… That's a Rampant Rabbit,' Arse says smugly, loving the fact that she's got the answer correct. As if she's in school or something.

'Well, actually,' Mary's make-up face skews a little to the left before returning to the centre, 'this is another model. Different. Made especially for us at Lovelife.com.' Mary looks at me briefly after saying dot com.

'Like a copy, is it?' I ask.

'Not at all,' says Mary, a little flustered, 'this is called a Swivelling Squirrel and it does so much more than any other vibrator. It swivels and burrows its way …' and I feel myself tightening up as she says it. Burrows! I mean, burrows?! She hasn't got the best grip on the English language considering she wants to sell me something that's supposed to go inside me. I try not to laugh, because I still sort of feel for her.

'And you've got an offer on today, 'ave you Mary?'

Mam is tryin' her hardest to be kind to her. Her friend Hannah is friends with Mary and she knows a bit about her past, so she's bein' gentle.

'I don't reckon it's different to the Rampant Rabbit myself,' I say, because it does look exactly the same. 'I'd be careful with copyright if I were you. I saw this programme once. A spin-off of *Dragon's Den*, it was. These people got twenty years.'

Mary's struggling now, and I feel a bit guilty for saying what I've just said. It's the wine it is, lettin' my mouth run away with me. It's just that I'd been given the impression that she was goin' to be able to give me a run for my money. Her hard, made-up face. Her sexual prowess. Her words and her confidence in part one of the performance. But now, to be honest, I'm not so sure. Mary and Mam have a bit of a conversation, so Arse and me get a chance for a quick natter.

'Fun, fun, fun,' Arse says before launching in, 'd'you remember Gwen bein' slow with some words?'

'She still can't say tomato.'

'Perry can't get to some things he means. Can't get things out.'

'Don't worry, mun. The moment he gets to school, he'll catch up like nothin' you've ever seen. They pick it all up from other kids. Nothin' to do with the teachers.'

'You reckon?'

'Definite.' I send her all the hope I can. 'Pen-pridd's a really good school.'

She nods, but I can tell there's some kind of problem.

'Alan don't think they should go to Welsh school. 'Specially if Perry's strugglin' with English.'

A hellish disappointed feelin' washes over me. Just then, Mary shoves the squirrel in my face. 'What d'you think? Suitable girth? You're welcome to touch it. Go on Sam love, give it a stroke!'

Mam laughs, hammered on white wine.

'Come on, mun, girls! Let's get SHAGGIN'!' Mary swings the disgusting squirrel in the air just as the song 'Girls Just Want to Have Fun' starts blarin'.

'Samantha!' Mary squeaks and then laughs at the way she's just said it. 'Ooh! Excuse me! Samantha – ewer turn to be the guinea pig. Or should I say, the squirrel. Come up by 'ere with Mary to switch the squirrel on and feel it squiverin'!'

Mam laughs out loud again, but I'm not in the mood no more. Not that I ever was. Mary's starin' at me, all eyes and eyeshadow and pink dust.

'Sam! Sam!' Mam chants on her own, havin' a bloody brilliant old time. Glad of the distraction from our conversation, Arse claps too. Mary's getting hyper now. Determined to get me on the 'stage' with her. But it's my fuckin' lounge. The thudding of the music really beginning to get to me.

I take a look around. My sofa's pushed back. My telly's turned towards the wall. The pole that Mary's brought (to show us how pole dancing can help you lose a stone in the space of a month) sticks out like a sore thumb. I suddenly feel like I'm on a cheap television set. Or even on a spaceship.

'Sami! Come up here and treat ewer fanny!' Mary is in doubles laughing about how clever she's just been. And to be fair, even though I'm totally pissed off as this fairground whizzes around in my lounge, I do think it's amazing that she's just managed to rhyme off the top of her head. Must have been luck.

Mary leans towards me, all sexy and weird and tries to pull me up again. But I strank. I can't help myself.

'Just leave me alone will ew, woman!'

She immediately pulls back, drops the Squirrel to the floor and looks all limp and useless. Now, to be fair on me, it's not as if I've sworn at her or been really rude, but my shouting seems to have completely got to her. Mam's face drops. Arse just sits there, dyin' to go out for a fag and escape whatever's about to kick off.

Before I know it, Mary's sitting on the chair. Her hands cradling her head. All that make-up, I'm thinking to myself, bein' smudged by her sweaty sex-palms.

'You alright, love?' Music still blarin', Mam creeps across the carpet on her knees, still carrying her white wine.

I look at Arse and do big eyes. This situation has kind of overtaken our conversation about Pen-pridd school, but I can tell where it's headed. They're not gonna go to a Welsh school, and Alan's obviously still a control freak and a prick.

We all creep closer. Kneel on the floor. Look up at the

big pink blancmange with matchstick legs. And then she shows her face again. She's covered in tears. Mary, the thirty-minute sex bomb. It's as if it's struck midnight and she's lost all her powers. She looks at my Mam, mascara streaming over her cheekbones like ink cartridges. She must have a month's supply on.

'It can never be as bad as that,' Mam says with love all over her words. 'Sam didn't mean nothin' by it. She's just a tincy bit frigid, that's all.' I look over at her with disgust. What the hell?

Mary ignores Mam and sighs a deep sigh which gives me an indication as to how huge her lungs must be.

'I know there's somethin' else the matter, love,' Mam says all carin' and sweet like the Mam-to-everyone she's always been. 'Hannah told me you've had it rough.'

Just then, the 'Pretty Woman' song comes on and Mam tells me to switch it off. Only as soon as I do, it's uncomfortably quiet here. All weird and muted. Even Mary, weepin' in silence. I try and get rid of my guilt. Convinced by now that the slightest thing would have set this woman off tonight. A slam of a door, even.

'I can't do this no more. I'm useless.' Mary says, all pathetic, like a child.

'Come on now,' Mam says in warm tones, 'you were brilliant!'

'You heard about my brother, did you?' She unsexily wipes her nose with her bare-naked arm. Mam pats Mary's left thigh. Then, without even looking at me, she says, 'Go and fetch Mary a tissue.'

As I get up, I spare a thought for little Gwen, hoping she's fast asleep and far away from all this shit.

'I have heard what he did, yes.' Mam sighs. 'Then again, we've all got members of the family who do strange things …'

I sit there, wonderin' what Mam's on about.

'Our Gareth, see,' Mam goes on, and I cringe at the thought of her tellin' family business just in order to make someone else feel better about their lives, 'he's been ill with us. Went to Iraq, didn't he. D'you remember Hannah sayin'?' Mary nods. 'And he was awful bad in the head for a while after that. He'd seen things, see. And he got admitted, didn't he, Sam, because he went beserk one afternoon …' and I look away because of the openness of it.

'But Gareth was servin' his country,' Mary says. 'Paul was messin' with animals.'

'I know,' Mam says quickly as my mouth drops open, 'but swings and roundabouts, isn't it, love? Swings and roundabouts.'

'Point is, we've all got things to deal with,' adds Mam. 'Things you have to put in the back of ewer mind. Things you have to try and forget in order to move on,' and for a moment I actually feel as if Mam's talking about her baby that didn't come. And about the fact that Dad's in jail. And about the divorce.

'And the thing is, right, the moral of the story I'm tryin' to tell ew, see. Gareth's fit as a fiddle now. I mean, granted, he's a changed man, but he's back on his feet.

Workin'. Got his own bakery. Point bein', and this is it see, everythin' always sorts itself out. And I know, I know it's embarrassing for your family. And your poor old Mam. And I understand that her cocker spaniel was involved. But the point being is that He'll. Get. Better. You mark my words. And people *will* forget.'

'I'll never forget,' Mary says, with a look that tells me that she's scared of the fact that they're from the same blood.

'But other people will, see. Chips, isn't it.'

A confused Mary rubs her eyes, making the mascara situation even worse. Of course, I know exactly what's comin' next. She's always used this expression with me.

'Today's news ...' and she doesn't finish the sayin', leavin' Mary out on barren land without a clue how that's supposed to offer her solace.

'Got to be thankful for what you've got is the point,' Arse says even though that's nothing at all to do with the saying in hand. She fills Mary's glass to the brim and smiles pathetically. I don't know what it is about the sound of wine being poured. It just goes through me. Arse passes Mary the glass. 'You got a husband?'

'Yes,' says Mam, on Mary's behalf. 'Yes, she has, and he's handsome.' I admire the way she's propping her up, helping her out. 'He was in my class in school. We all wanted to touch his skin because it was olive skin see. Olive skin. All lovely and soft.'

Mam carries on, determined.

'And ewer so gorgeous. Look at you. All pretty in pink. And you've got this lovely job,' Mam goes that step too far and sets the blancmange off again. She starts weepin' into the wine and Arse rolls her eyes at me. Precisely, I think to myself. Pre-bloody-cisley. We've paid thirty quid each for this honour. If it wasn't such a rip-off, I'd laugh my tits off.

'I can't do it right,' Mary says pathetically and I feel my shoulders sag to the ground. 'I'm not sexy enough to do Lovelife.com.'

'Oh, come on now Mary, you are damn well sexy. You're a sex pussy!' Mary looks at her in shock.

'Kitten, Mam, not pussy,' but Mam doesn't even look at me.

'I know what I meant, Sam.'

'The youngsters don't think I'm sexy no more,' Mary says, pointing over towards Arse and me. We're secretly quite chuffed we've been called youngsters, but I feel a duty to contribute now. God, she's manipulative.

'I do,' I say limply, 'you are sexy.'

'Ewer just sayin' it,' Mary says with hiccups, 'to be nice.'

'No, you are,' Arse says, like a shit extra in a cheap film, 'a woman's sexy all through her life, mun,' and I kind of believe she means that.

But despite our efforts, Mary's still cryin'. Mam looks desperate now. Drunk. Nearly mental. 'Oh come on mun, love, stop it now.'

'I've spoilt ewer party,' she mumbles, all spit and

teeth, 'and there was you phonin' me to come and cheer up ewer daughter.' Mary looks at Mam and Mam looks at me. I suddenly feel a bit pathetic too.

Mam gets up from the carpet, and with a determined look in her eyes, she grabs the Swivelling Squirrel. Holding it in the air like a baton, she raises her voice. 'Mary. Stand up!'

Mary stands up with the strength of Mam's command. You daren't refuse her. Not when she's like this.

Mam looks through the window. 'D'you see down there? Sam-by-there's aunty is in an Old People's Home, just down by the rugby pitch.' Mary looks out at Pontypridd. 'She'd do anything to be with us now, discussing this Snarlin' Squirrel …'

'Swivelling,' I correct her.

Mam ignores me. 'But she can't, can she? 'Cos she's on a one-way road to death.' Friggin' hell, Mam, I think to myself. If Anti Peg heard her talking like this she'd whack her one.

'This is our time to talk dirty, Mary. Before we dry up like prunes. We need to fiddle with our fannies. Have fun!' Arse is holding onto my arm by now. Confused and a little bit scared of the middle-aged revolution that's kickin' off in my lounge.

'Move them hips, girl. Go on! Wiggle 'em!' Mary looks at Mam. Dumbfounded. 'Come ON mun!' Mam says with a squeak. 'Bloody well wiggle those hips and think of Wales. Bloody hell woman, you're only in your forties!'

'I'm thirty-seven,' Mary says quietly.

'Young and sexy! Wiggle 'em, come on! Wiggle them hips,' and suddenly Mary's wiggling back and forth.

'And don't you let no youngsters make you think that they've got the right on sex! Because they haven't! They're fumblers! They haven't got a friggin' clue what they're doin'. D'you want to know how old I was when I had my first orgasm?'

'Mam,' I say firmly. This is too far. I don't know what's gotten into her.

'You're right! They're fumblers!' Mary screams in agreement, getting some weird release from it all.

'My man Terry tells me I go like a steam roller on Red Bull!' And Mary screams, 'RED BULL!' at the top of her voice.

'Mam, mun! Stop it.'

'No, Sam! It's about time you realise! Us women, our age! We love it! We want it!'

'OUR AGE!' Mary screeches in happiness and I begin to really question her intelligence.

'Gwen's sleepin', Mam,' and as soon as I've said it, Mam seems to sober up.

Only it isn't Mam we need to worry about by now. It's Mary. I watch her as she reaches for her glass of wine, downing it in one. A trickle of wine dribbles down her chin as she grabs holds of the Swivelling Squirrel, thumping it into the air like a crazed animal.

'Sex! Sex! Sex!' she shouts at the top of her voice, moving her hips back and forth. We just stare at her. This woman who came all the way here so that we could tell her that she's sexy. This woman who's dancing without music. Swinging her hips to a tune in her head.

♥

Half an hour later, and Mam and Mary are having a secret debrief in the kitchen. And somehow or other, I'm the proud owner of a Swivelling Squirrel. I bought it out of pity in the end. Pity and fear. Arse, on the other hand, bought some fanny putty. She doesn't know what it is, but she reckons it'll be fine in her hair if it doesn't work out anywhere else.

I can't help but wonder whether this was all a part of Mary from Lovelife.com's marketing ploy. Breaking down and emotionally blackmailing customers into buyin' things for the sake of her mental wellbeing. Ploy or no ploy, I have no intention of using something that looks as if it could do a great deal of damage if it was on full speed.

'Strange night all-in-all,' Arse says, checkin' her phone and then throwing it back into her bag.

'Aye,' I say, looking at my best friend, knackered by the whole bleedin' palaver.

Just then Mam rushes in from the kitchen, her hair catchin' up with her a few moments later.

'It's Molly, love,' she says all out of breath and flustered, 'she's goin' into labour. Mary's just gone to fetch some towels.'

Find Me

I'm cleanin' up after breakfast when the doorbell rings. It seems like only five minutes ago I watched Gwen climb into that-man-Terry's car ready for school. She didn't want to go today, what with the new puppies in town. But I eventually got her to go. Watched her from the window, walkin' towards his car with her little lunchbox. Her blond hair like gold against the grey of the concrete buildings.

I answer in my dressin' gown and it's him. Richard. I knew he'd call some time, knew he'd come lookin' for somethin'.

'Can I come in?'

I try to shut the door but he stops it from closing, just in time. I had a feeling he might do that. Only I don't want him to think he can come in that easy.

'You're the one who texted me.'

I take a good look at him. My daughter's Dad. For a moment I catch myself thinking about the years we had together and the fact that his *X-Files* boxset is still on top of the DVD player.

'Cup of tea?'

But he doesn't deserve one. Not after everything.

'I'm workin' in the caff in an hour, and I've promised I'll go and see Peg before that.'

'Quarter of an hour …' he says, putting his hands

back in his trouser pockets. Red Adidas joggers. The ones he knows I hate. 'You can afford the time to have a cup of tea.'

And just like that, I open the door. Because I'm weak, and because I always knew I would. This poky flat is closing in on me as we squeeze our bodies along the corridor. As he walks towards the kitchen, Molly sees him, and gets annoyingly excited.

'Oh my God, pups. Crazy!'

'Don't wind her up,' I say coldly, 'she might stand on the babies.'

'Alright,' Richard says, obviously wantin' to please me. 'Gwen in school?'

I don't answer. Where the hell else would she be?

'She okay?'

I nod my head, and pull the string of my dressing gown tighter, just like Mam does. I sort of catch myself playing 'house' for a minute, I think it's a coping mechanism.

'How long you gonna keep this up? It's over. I told you.' He comes closer. I smell toothpaste. 'We all make mistakes mun, Sam.'

I just look at him. This man I grew to love.

'The band's getting back together, by the way,' he says, only I don't respond.

He kneels down towards Molly. 'I thought you'd be glad I'd be able to give you some cash. Chief reckons we're tight now ...'

'Chief reckons a lot of fuckin' things. Now if you don't

mind, I better change for work. Someone's got to pay the bills.'

I close the bedroom door and start changing. Knickers, socks, trousers, minging red T-shirt. Then I hear the door of the bedroom creak. And I know he's come in. I turn around and there he is. He walks towards me. And it's not that I want it to happen. It's just like second nature.

'I'm changin', mun.'

'I miss you,' he says with his eyes wide open, and I believe him. He has nowhere to hide the lies. His lids are as far up as they can go.

'Shut up, is it.' Only I don't mean it, and he knows that.

Then he comes even closer, like we both knew he would from the start.

♥

We lie side by side on the bed. He's bright enough to know that this doesn't mean he's allowed to come back. He's bright enough to understand that I want him, and want rid of him. He won't try to hug me. And I won't try and hug him. It's not like that any more. It's like something I can't put my finger on. A strange love. And it kills me. 'Cos I'm bright enough to know better. I'm bright enough to know that all I feel after the brief happiness is hurt. All I want to do is rub it out with a rubber, erase it with an eraser pen like I used to do with shit sentences in school. And it's my own fault. I've set up some rules, and now I'm not obeying them. Rebellin' against my own self.

'Remember the mingin' pizza?' I watch him staring up at the ceiling, tryin' to woo me with stupid stories from a time gone by. Our first dates. The past we'll always share, regardless of everything that's changed now.

I don't answer him because I know what he's trying to do. And then he does what he does best. He amuses me. Reminds me that we've always been friends.

'You better get to sortin' that crack in the wall. Be able to see out soon.'

'You're such a twat, you do know that, don't you?' I say with a smirk and some breath.

'Can't help it,' he places one hand behind his neck, until I can see the smooth white of his inner arms. I remember some psychologist saying once that when someone puts their arms on their heads in a meeting, or behind their heads, or up above, they think that they're in complete control. I get up. Don't let him indulge any longer.

Just then he helps himself to the Love Hearts on the side cabinet. I snatch them away from him, but he's already got one. Chomping on it straight away.

'You didn't even check to see what it said.' He smiles, revealing another one in his hand. The sugary words are pressing up against his palm as I zip up and sort myself ready for work. I try not to look like I'm bothered, even though I'm wondering whether the message he's holding has any clue for our future. That's how childish I am.

'D'you remember when we nearly went and got married? In Anglesey?'

I ignore him. Because thinking about it makes my belly hurt.

'Should have done it. I would have done the vows in Welsh and all.'

'You don't speak Welsh.'

'Never too late,' he says then, crunching on another Love Heart. Swallowing it down with no idea what it said on it. Annoyed, I pull him from the bed.

'Right, you. Out!'

His eyes want this to mean something. Only I can't let it. I want to believe him that this can all be different, only all of my life experiences are telling me different.

'Mam said something that you've had a revamp up the caff. Glanville forkin' out for once is he?'

'Ta-ra Richard,' I say, staring him square in the face, 'shut the door on your way out.'

Cheeky Girl

On my way to see Peg before work, I spot Gareth. My head's full of nonsense after what's just happened and so I'm not really in the mood to see him.

'Yo, yo, sis!' he semi-shouts (there really wasn't any need for a semi-shout).

'Gotta go,' I say, 'I'm late. I gotta visit Peg.' I carry on walkin', but he chases after me.

'Ow, wait up. Anj and me've been thinkin'. You and Gwen wanna come up for tea tomorrow night? 'Cos we've got somethin' we want to tell you.'

I stop. Turn towards him, don't say a word. 'She's not pregnant. It's somethin' else. Somethin' more excitin'.'

His red cheeks turn redder, and for the first time ever in his life he actually looks like a baker. In actual fact, he looks like something straight out of a storybook. 'Bread of Heaven', I keep thinking. Hellish original name for a bakery, Gar.

I try hard to remember what he's just asked me.

'Alright. We'll come for a bit, but we can't stay long,' and he smiles. Get lost, I think. Maybe life's alright for you, but it's fuckin' tough for some people. Sayin' that, it kind of gives me hope. The fact that he's been so down with it all, and the fact that he's all fat and smug now. It shows you how journeys go. And anyway, Gareth has always been like that. He's a twat when he's at his happiest and he's nice when he's low. So I'd rather hate him, if you get my drift.

♥

She's made an extra special effort today. Gone to town with the eyeshadow. It looks as if half the coal from the mines is sitting on her lids.

She coughs.

'See him,' she points with her nose towards one of the old boys, paralytic-seemin', slumped deep into the brown faux-leather chair.

'Shagged him last week. Hell of a goer.' I just give her a look.

'And how's little Gwen?' she asks, with a twinkle in her eye. In the background, Sue and Emily Jones are havin' a huge scrap. It's just like bein' in a crèche, I swear.

'Gwen's fine. What about you, have you been takin' ewer medication like ewer s'posed to?'

'Ewer Dad called on the phone yesterday,' she says, ignoring my question. I hate the way Dad pops up in conversation. He has the knack of comin' and goin' like he bloody well pleases. A bit like Madonna in the charts. And, even more like Madonna in the charts, when he comes back, no one's quite sure why he bothered in the first place.

'And work, how's work? Is that boss of yours still a prick?'

I nod, because I can't even be arsed to go into Glanville's latest antics. The man with no clue how to run a café.

'Has anything fun been goin' on up here, then?'

Peg's black hairsprayed hair shudders. 'As you know, this place is fuckin' party central.' A wave of guilt washes over me. What a stupid question to ask. I can see a few commodes hidin' behind the armchairs. There's only *that* much fun you can have sittin' on your arse all day, waitin' to die.

'Try and entertain myself I do. Masturbation and stuff.' Peg smiles a toothless smile. I wonder where her gnashers are for a moment, but then I notice that they've fallen onto her lap. She's laughin' now, like a real fool. Husky laugh. Naughty.

'Peg, mun, shut the fuck up,' I bark through a semi-closed mouth, 'some of the oldies are sleepin'.'

I pick up the teeth. They feel all hard, wet and warm. I offer them back to her but she refuses, her forehead goin' all stubborn.

'Put them back in ewer head, mun,' I demand, but I don't want to draw attention to myself.

'I pancy one ob the myrses, see,' even though she has no teeth in, I can just about make out what she's talkin' about.

'You haven't turned lezza, 'ave ew?' Acting I am, to make her laugh. I push the teeth hard into her mouth and she jiggles them about a bit with her tongue.

'Lesbian?' she questions, her teeth back in place. 'I

haven't done tits and fanny for years, mun. I like that song, mind. "I kissed a girl and I liked it".' Peg smiles and starts singing, laughin' and splutterin' all over the place.

'Keep it down, is it?' She's definitely worse than she was. Cheekier. Dirtier.

'That song was written about me. I bet you'd never think that.'

I smile at her. Maybe a little condescending. Only she smiles back.

'Oooh, you young ones. You don't think we were up to nothin' before you were born, do you? Hilarious.'

I look at her. Tiny in that big brown chair. All you can see, really, are her clothes. Her body lost in them.

'You should be receivin' some royalties soon then. If that song was written about you.'

'Didn't write it, did I. You dick.' And that's me put in my place again. Time and time again. Just as Peg is about to carry on talking, a nurse comes in. A male nurse wearing an apron and brown shiny shoes like two chocolate bars. Peg taps me in the shins. Only it's more like a kick and it kills.

'It's him,' she whispers loudly. Practically speaking, actually. 'Jonathan. He's the nurse I fancy.' He is quite good-lookin', to be fair. Checkin' up on all the oldies. Makes him even cuter somehow.

'Peg keepin' you entertained, then?' he asks with a mischievous smile on his face. I'm about to answer him, but Peg gets the better of me.

33

'Not as entertained as *you* will be when I get hold of you tonight.'

He smiles again. A bit vacant this time, as if he hasn't heard a thing.

'He fuckin' well wants me,' she brushes her black hair back. 'It's not about age, see, it's about personality. Compatibility.'

I know she's talkin' bollocks, but Peg has a really funny way of makin' you feel as if everythin' she says could be for real.

'And this,' she says, pullin' out her false teeth and popping them back in, 'means I give the best head in the world.'

I shake my head, hoping to God that the nurse guy hasn't heard a thing. Then, I stand up ready to leave. Peg yawns and shows her pink tongue, her back molars and her silver fillings. She reminds me a lot of Molly. And her little pups. I swear my mind's fucked up sometimes.

As I leave her, I can't help but imagine her later on tonight, leanin' over and givin' that Jonathan a blow job. His dark eyes. Her gnashers on the side table. I want to erase it from my memory. I really do. Only, like everything, the more I try to push it to the back of my mind, the more it keeps comin' back. Like a hideous, very niche porn film.

LUCKY DAY

I knew that something was cooking with my boss Glanville when he started goin' on and on about the fact that Campanini's up the road was doin' better than us. And then, lo and behold, a few weeks back, he comes in one morning like a little Oompa-loompa, full of the joys of spring, with a special announcement.

'Girls. Something momentous 'as 'appened. I've found out, no word of a lie, that I'm Italian.'

Credit crunch does funny things to a man, aye. Apparently (and I'm stressing this apparently, because basically it's COMPLETE AND UTTER FUCKING RUBBISH), he'd been searching back through his family tree and he'd 'discovered' that he had a great-great-GREAT grandfather from the north of Italy. Fucking hell, I remember thinkin' at the time, I'm probably more closely related to the Queen.

'Where's the surname, 'en?' I asked that morning with my eyebrows all scrunched together.

'My Italian surname hasn't survived the family line.' Short-arse was wearing black trousers, a white shirt and strangely new slicked-back dark hair.

'Come to think of it,' said Pauline, lickin' his arse to the high heavens, 'you do look a bit Italian.'

'Really?' I mutter. And Glanville throws me a look.

Needless to say, I'm not at all surprised as I turn up

today to see that he's obviously been decorating over the weekend. Framed black and white photos of Italian families dotted around the room.

All twenty stone of Carol is takin' up half the kitchen. She's looking over at Pauline, who's doin' the tuna mayonnaise. Talkin' at her as she always does. Blabbin' away about a signed photo of Les Dennis she's hopin' to get valued. Pauline's mixing all the tuna up like cement and putting it in a big plastic container under the glass. Old tuna mayonnaise and new tuna mayonnaise all mixed up together now, all shiny underneath the yellow lights and the glass. Then, she just stares at the stuff, looking as if she wants to jump into it. Fill her ears up with mayo so as not to hear Carol bangin' on. Small girl is Pauline. All petite with mousey brown hair. Ordinary looking, but with a really pretty cupid mouth. Her lips always seem really red, even though she doesn't wear lipstick. She's got a weird chin too, has Pauline. Kind of like a bum.

I get to making myself a cup of tea and I sort out a few of the mugs.

'Watch them mugs now,' blurts Carol. 'I put them in order this mornin'.'

I'm close enough to Carol now to see all the lines and the hairs on her face. I imagine bein' her husband, wakin' up to her every mornin'. Her big green eyes, her lumpy lookin' nose, and her heavy upper lip. For a moment I'm completely addicted to looking at the area of skin between her lip and her nose. She seems to have a very long one of those, whatever they're called. Long, long, as if it went on forever.

'Has Glanville put our shifts out yet?' Pauline lifts her head up from the mayonnaise like a nervous bird. She nods awkwardly and lowers her head down again, staring at the fillings.

I head for the boiler room. Want to see for myself. It smells like old trainers in the boiler room. Always has and always will. Pinned to the noticeboard with a red drawing pin is the rota. I study it. Notice that everyone's got fewer shifts than usual. I head straight back into the kitchen area.

'We haven't got half as much shifts!' My throat dries up, spit disappearing from my mouth as if it doesn't want to get involved in this dispute. I look at Pauline.

'He's putting two on every day instead of three,' she says. Mayonnaise eyes down.

I pick up my cuppa and storm out through the back. I can't hack it. I need fresh air. I know I've only just got here, but tough. Leaning against the back wall in the drizzle, sipping my tea, I can feel my trousers soaking up the wet. I reach into my pinny for my fags. Moments later, I swallow the smoke down until my belly's full. Full of grey-black smoke. What am I goin' to do with one or two shifts in a fortnight? I may as well be on the dole. I stare into my cup of tea.

Suddenly the back door creaks.

Please don't be Carol. Please don't be Carol.

'Listen,' Pauline's voice slides around the place like a

bar of soap in the drizzle. The kind of voice you can't quite focus on. 'Glanville's tryin' his best.' Her eyes are still full of mayonnaise. Obviously. A gluey, garlicky conjunctivitis. She'd make excuses for a mass murderer would Pauline. It's just her style.

'Come off it, will you? The only person he tries his best for is himself.' The drizzle and the cold really beginning to get to me, 'I've got enough on my plate as it is, without all this shit.'

Pauline sighs.

'Ewer much brainier than us lot, mun. You shouldn't even be here.'

'Is it? Where exactly should I be then?'

We both stand in silence for a while until it cringes me out.

'Carol's like rent-a-mouth today in'she?'

'Harold left her over the weekend.' Pauline's eyes are wide open. Her mascara lashes framin' her tiny little eyes. 'Bit shit really.'

A steady stream of guilt flows into my belly, setting like concrete. I always remember her saying she was a big woman because she ate with Harold. She cooked for him, ate with him, ate for him, did everything for him. And now look what he's gone and done. Bloody well gone. Leavin' her too out of breath to come after him.

'Right,' I say then, because there's nothing else to say. Pauline smiles a sad smile and slides back indoors. Mouthin' away because she's hurtin' like hell. That's our Carol. Should have known something was up, really.

I step back into the café and I'm instantly greeted with his annoying excuse for a face. Only it's worse than usual. Because he's enthused about somethin' again. Goin' off on one like a garden gnome on acid.

'Good afternoon, girls!' he says excitedly. 'Gather round, gather ROUND!'

Carol lifts her head from her dinner, still chompin' with her mouth open. Pauline heads over. I do too, reluctantly. I watch him as he fusses over some bits of paper. Spreads them out on the table. Like a lawyer or a magician. Carol stares up at him. His eyes are bulgin' out now. Licking up the words he's written with a Bic biro. Lips getting plumper, shiny wet with spit.

'Here's the embryonic stages of the new menu!' His upper lip curls up a bit to the left like Elvis. 'You are gonna LOVE this!'

His emphasis on some words makes me feel sick. I look at my watch. Ten minutes of this. I can afford to listen to ten minutes of this. Then, I'm gonna have to murder him with my own bare hands.

'Don't laugh now, right. But somethin' a bit funny happened to me last night. I had this kind of "experience". Talkin' to … well, I suppose you could say to the dead, really. As if my ancestors all decided to channel stuff through me. Feedin' me with information. Like I was a laptop.'

I stare at him. He must be clinically insane. Either that or he thinks we are dull.

'What you on about now, Glan?' Carol asks, pickin'

a bit of stringy chicken from the gap between her front teeth.

'See, thing is, right, this mornin' when I woke up, Theresa informed me that I had been sweatin' profusely all through the night! Like a pig! Imagine that.'

I can't believe he's doin' this. He's such a berk. He's the kind of man who uses so many words that in the end he makes the art of communication feel pointless, and even depressing. He takes the value out of things. Piles words on top of each other until they don't mean shit.

'And then it comes to me see. That's what it is! It's as if all the Italian blood in me is comin' alive again. Conjuring in me. Like Johnny Depp in *Message to a Vampire*. And I had to run downstairs, girls! Like a cheetah, I was. Runnin' through the jungle. I looked about for some paper and a pen. I tell you, it was like some kind of message from above. I just wrote out the new menu. Flowin' through me it was. I was like a medium. Takin' down the information. In a flash. And bish, bash, bosh. Out it came.'

'Give us a look then,' says Carol unexcitedly as she reaches across the table. She holds a corner of the paper, but he snatches it back from her just in time. It's as if he's a primary school kid. Actually, I'm not givin' Gwen enough credit.

'A master never reveals, you know, he doesn't tell people …' and he's stuck. He doesn't even remember the rest of the line. I notice that white spit has gathered in the corners of his mouth. Proper mingin', and one of the things I loathe most about humans.

'Come on mun, Glan,' Pauline's obviously excited. In fact, I think this might be the single most excitin' thing that's happened to Pauline this year. No. That might be unfair. Then again …

Glanville coughs. Clears his throat. Stands tall.

'Okay, then, girls. Okay, well, this is how it sounds. It's different, mind, there's no denyin' it. And it's a bit exotic, like. And don't get scared by some of the words I use now 'cos it'll ALL become clear.'

Now I must admit, even *I'm* a little bit intrigued by now. I mean, I watch a lot of these cookin' type programmes. And food does make me excited. Because of Gareth, probably. I mean, I even knew that that bish, bash, bosh business he just said comes from Jamie Oliver.

'We will be serving,' he announces, 'the followin' Italian cuisine in … Caffeteria Glanvillas.'

He looks about for adoring glances. I stifle a laugh.

'An array of paninis, girls. Bread, that is. From Italy.' We all stare at him blankly, not supposed to say that we've all been up Campanini's to get one every Wednesday since last Christmas. Pauline is nodding keenly by now. She is SUCH a CREEP.

'Ice-cream, girls. Very Italian cuisine.' My lids are heavy now, each little black lash judgin' how many brain cells he has in that head of his. I don't usually like that side of me. The way I judge people without them knowing. Only this time, I think it's justifiable.

'And then, the piece de lal resistence is this, right ... A TAPAS corner.'

'Isn't that Spanish?' Carol asks, her lower lip hangin' loose from her face. I nod because Carol's bloody right.

'Does it really matter that much, girls?'

We all look at him and happen to answer at the same time with a resounding 'Yes'. He looks at Carol first.

'It's nothin' to be frightened of, Carol. Tapas is food to be embraced. It's all about the sharin' with Italian, see. Loving. Hugging. Eating together ...'

'We've got an Italian caff already,' Carol says, pushin' her plate away, 'plus, tapas is Spanish. People know that kind of stuff these days. 'Cos of *Masterchef*. And Morrisons.'

'Splittin' hairs now, in'ew, Carol? Little bits of food is what tapas is. People choosing what they do want on their plate. Beans. Chips. Sausages. Sun-dried tomatoes.'

'Serve all that already,' answers Carol, 'except for the sun-drip tomatoes, which no one would want anyway.'

'Well. We're gonna go far with that attitude, in'we Carol?' I glance towards Pauline. Glanville seriously isn't going to give in. 'All I'm talkin' about by 'ere is givin' people choice. Choice is the king of the twenty-first century. Don't you read the papers? So if people want sun-dried tomatoes, beans, squid and olives, they can have it. In Glanvillas.'

'Yeah, but no one will,' Carol closes her mouth. Clenches her jaw.

'Isn't squid …?' Pauline cuts across everyone, in a world of her own.

'Yes it is, Pauline, it's octopus,' says Glanville. Proud.

Pauline cocks her head to the side like a dog. 'People round here are not going to be up for that, Glan.'

'Look. Forget the squid. Point is …'

'This is goin' to be a disaster,' says Carol, staring up at the ceiling.

'Girls. Listen. This is the Italian way of thinkin'. Give the customer what he or she wants. Tapas means they can have whatever the HELL they WANT …'

'What if they want olives, beans and ice-cream?' asks Carol.

'Give them olives, beans and ice-cream!' Glanville looks as if he's just delivered a historical quote.

We all look at him. Expressionless.

'Look, ' he has a new air about him all of a sudden. 'I'm not expecting you to understand all this now. These are BIG changes. All I'm asking, for the time bein', is that you look at the menus. Think about the ingredients,' he breathes deeply, 'and practise ewer Italian.'

'What?' Carol's face scrunches up. She shifts about in her chair. 'I don' even speak *Welsh*, let alone *Italian*.'

'Tapas is Spanish. This is never gonna work,' I say matter-of-factly. Even though I think we've all accepted that point.

'Spanish, Italian, Portuguese. What does it matter? In the grand scheme of things? It's the Mediterranean, innit? The taste of the Middle East. D'you think the

Romans sat down and had conversations about tiny little things like this when they took over China?'

I bite my tongue. Nearly hundred percent sure that he's mixing up two different programmes he's watched on the History Channel.

As soon as the speech comes to an end, Pauline and Carol wander back to base, mutterin' under their breath. I, on the other hand, stick to Glanville like glue. He's sitting down on a chair now and the chairs are stuck to the floor, so even though I'm sure he'd like to move it closer to the table to get some privacy, he just can't.

'Can I have a word please?'

He doesn't look up, he's chewing on one of his knuckles, makin' minor changes to the menu with a Bic biro.

'Shifts,' I say. 'I haven't got hardly any this fortnight.'

He looks up now. Knows he's going to have to deal with this one. Even puts down his biro.

'Everyone's bein' cut down, Sam. Durin' this interim period. Let's see how we get on once this new menu's in place, is it?' Despite myself, I nod. Even though the only thing I really fancy doing is sticking that Bic as far up his nostril as I can physically get it.

As I walk away, I kick myself. You better be right or you're goin' to regret it, is what I should have said. 'Cos that's what my character would have said in a film. I swear, I'd be one hell of a woman if I managed to be more quick off the mark. A force to be reckoned with. I swear.

Cool Kid

I'm standing there with all the other Mams, waitin' for mine to come out. To come out and look up, searching for a familiar face. And suddenly, here she comes. And here come all the others too. All chatter and shoes and laces on the concrete. Dragging bags and open lunch boxes behind them. I spot her searching for me amongst the other Mams. And then she finds me, a look of disappointment spreading over her face because I'm not that-man-Terry. That-man-Terry's face denotes a fun ride back. A Wagon Wheel. Singing 'Killer Queen' with the windows down, even when it's raining. But when he's not about, we walk home. Because we haven't got no flashy wheels. All we've got is our hoods and the shoes on our feet.

As she waves goodbye to the other girls and boys in red jumpers I grab her red satchel. She sighs heavily as if the weight of the world is on her shoulders.

'What's wrong, love?' I ask. 'D'you wanna piggy back?'

Gwen doesn't answer, only swings her long arms back and forth like an orang-utang, swallowing the road up with her legs in broad, tomboy steps. The normality of her makes me feel sane again. The regularity she brings me is mesmerising.

'Just to tell you, Mam, I'm going out to play tonight,' she stomps the ground, pushing the concrete pavement deeper into the earth.

'What about the puppies?'

'Have they got eyes now?' she asks excitedly, remembering about them.

'Aye,' I say, 'one or two of 'em got eyes, but Molly's really tired, so I was thinkin' maybe you could babysit them tonight. What d'you say? Give Molly a break?'

'Alright,' Gwen says with a groan, as if she's aware of her unavoidable responsibility towards the animals. As we head up the hill, past the house where I first saw the film *Arachnophobia*, I remember that I need to get us something for our tea.

'Mam's gonna have to pop in the Spar a minute.'

She pebble-dashes her words at me: 'Can I have sweets?'

I hold onto my purse. There'll obviously be enough for sweets, but I don't know whether there'll be much available for anything else.

'Fish fingers we're 'avin' tonight, alright? Fish finger sarnies.'

'I don't like fingers,' Gwen says, in a mood.

'You like fish mind, don't you … things like tuna. Remember?'

'Not fingers. Can't eat 'em when they look like fingers,' she says sulkily.

'But they don't, love, they don't look like fingers at all.' I'm becoming a bit annoyed with the whole discussion, so I just shut up.

The red and white Spar sign is in front of us now, and in truth, I really don't want to take her in. Inside is a world of things she could grab, nag and moan about. True to form, the moment we get in, she's off like a bolt of electricity up the aisle. I wave hello at Kez, who's standin' behind the counter, and try to mask the double-take I've just done by looking as if I'm majorly interested in the choice of batteries by her side. I don't know what she's done to her hair, but it's obvious she doesn't have a very honest relationship with her hairdresser.

Soon, as if it's second nature, I'm standin' by the cash machine. I put in my card, and take out a tenner even though I have to pay one pound fifty for the privilege. I'd take out more if I could, but I can't. Before you can say 'Love Hearts', Gwen's standing next to me. She holds up a small skull with the words 'Sherbet Skull' written on it in purple neon. I frown.

'No way you havin' that. It's cheap and nasty.'

Her lips curl down.

'It's Sherbet Skull, Mam. Everyone got 'em in school.'

I sense that this could lead onto hysterics. It's happened all too often in the past. So I just cave in. Like a damp sandcastle.

'Alright then, fine. But you're not havin' it before your tea, d'you hear me?'

Then just like that, the smile reappears. Miraculous, that. She should be in Hollywood, I swear.

♥

So she's lyin' in her bed and I'm sitting next to her. The curtains have been drawn but the light from the streetlamp outside is still trying to sneak in between the gaps. Her index finger is lodged deep inside the sour Sherbet Skull and her little pyjamas seem too small on her tonight.

'We're gonna have to get you new pyjamas, missus. Now have you brushed them teeth?' She nods through swathes of sherbet and spit-covered fingers.

'I told Molly and the babies a story,' she says, concentrating on getting more sherbet from the see-through skull.

'Did you? There's nice.'

'Told 'em a story about me and you and Dad goin' for a walk on the big mountain.'

I tuck her in, try to ignore what she's just said.

'Callum said today that ants can kill you,' she adds, discussing the most annoying individual in her classroom for the second night runnin', 'and he said his Dad's got a gun.'

'Story time,' I say, reaching for a little Welsh book from under the bed. I try my hardest to read her Welsh whenever I get a chance.

'He said, he went to the person who does the bins, "Watch out you, my Dad's got a gun. He can kill you".'

I smile at her, 'Callum's Dad's full of rubbish.' I reach for the Sherbet Skull. 'That's enough of that now. Story time, yeah? Wipe your hands here, see?'

'Don't want a story now,' her eyes narrow and nasty.

'Fine. Mam leave you now then, to go to sleep.'

I get up and plant a kiss on her fringe-forehead. She

sulks, pulling the quilt up over her head. I head for the door. Her tantrum suits me just fine, I'm bloody dyin' for a fag.

'Night night, now,' I whisper into the silence. 'Night night now, I said.'

A little voice cuts through the dark.

'Are you gonna be here in the morning?'

''Course I am,' I say, feeling the darkness flowing down my throat, into my belly.

'Promise?'

'Promise.'

'But Dad said that as well. And then he wasn't here.'

I stand there for a moment. No idea how to answer.

'You need to rest ewer head down. Not think about anything.'

'What can I think about?'

'Think about the puppies,' I try to sound light and lyrical. 'They're lyin' down with their Mam. Cwtshin' up, makin' little dog noises, with hardly no eyes. Ci bach yn gorwedd lawr. Yn cysgu. Yn breuddwydio.'

My Welsh sounds funny. 'Cos I hardly use it anymore.

'Yeah,' she says after a few seconds, breathing deeply, 'and Dad sittin' by the table too. Lookin' at them. Like this afternoon.'

'What d'you mean?' I ask, blind again in the darkness.

'I smelled him. He've been to see the puppies.'

'Nos da nawr, bach,' I sing, pulling the door after me.

'Don't shut it, Mam,' she shouts back. 'I want the light.'

So I leave it open.

REAL LOVE

Gwen's two hands are splayed across Gareth and Anj's fish tank as she peers through the glass, studying hundreds of pounds worth of tropical fish. Anj enters the lounge with a tray of mugs. I can't put my finger on it with her, but she's a bit annoyin'. It's as if she isn't ever really bein' herself.

'Coffee you said, wasn't it?'

She bloody well knows that's what I said.

'Two sugars, that's what you said, wasn't it?'

'How's everythin' up the Medical Centre?' Anj ignores my question, nervously looks over towards Gwen, who's wiping her after-school-fingers all over the glass.

'Gwen, love,' I say, 'leave the fishies alone, there's a good girl.'

'I'm only lookin,' she mumbles, lips against the glass. 'One by 'ere looks a bit dead.'

'Surgery's been a bit manic,' Anj says, finally. 'We had a few with explosive diarrhoea today. People getting piles with it and all. Can't even walk straight, some of them.'

'Oh, right.' I sip my coffee, wonderin' whether she's washed her hands since comin' home from work. 'And ewer Mam. How's she doin' now? After, you know, the op, like ...' Anj blushes for a moment.

'It's been ... well, it's sensitive, you know. She's doin' well, mind. But then it's difficult, isn't it? She can't drive.

She's not allowed to go swimmin'. And she loves her swimmin'.'

By now Gwen has got her hand in the fish tank.

'Gwen Elin Jones. Get that hand *out* of there. Some of those fishies are poison, in'they Anj?'

Anj nods, cool in her response.

'The scorpion fish could actually kill you. Yeah.'

Hearing this, I rush towards Gwen and drag her away from the tank. As I do so, one of her wet-skinned hands slaps against the glass. There's a moment of silence before she screams. Tears beginning to flood down her cheeks. Soon, she's sobbing. I drag her over to the cream sofa and sit her next to me. She's crossed her arms now. Angry with me.

'I'm sorry, love,' I say, but she's not listening. I can see the skin around her eyes is all red and blotchy. She's tryin' to catch her breath too. Popping her head higher every now and then in order to try and make room for more air.

'Went to see Peg yesterday,' Anj says then, before telling me a bit about the conversation they had. A flow of possessive emotion runs through me like ice water. It's as if she's tryin' to make herself all comfortable. Pushing her slippers into my family's slipper circle.

'Where's Gareth to then?'

'He's gettin' somethin' for you to see,' Anj says, mysteriously.

'Oh my God, you've bought a dog.'

Gwen's ears prick up, 'You got a dog?'

'No,' says Anj, 'no, no it's not a dog.' I'm so glad when

Gareth finally comes into the living room, I could cheer. How come it's such hard work to be in some people's company?

'What's this news then, bro?'

'Tell you now. Pizzas we've got. That alright?'

Gwen leans towards me, whispers in my ear. Looks rude, her doin' that, not sayin' what she wants to say out loud.

I look at Gareth, 'Gwen don't like bits on top of her pizza. Only plain.'

Gareth smiles at Gwen. 'They're all chicken and spinach, I think. They were on offer.'

Gwen looks particularly displeased and Gareth thinks on the spot. 'Uncle Gareth scrape it off for you, yeah?'

She nods, pulling her chin shyly towards her chest. I don't know why she's actin' like this – she knows Gareth well.

'So,' Gareth rubs his hands on his thighs nervously. Anj looks at him supportively. 'I wanted to tell you first. I haven't told Mam. Or Dad. But I'm gonna. Gonna go over the prison and everything.'

'Tell 'em what?' I ask, but he rambles on past me, his words like little ants pottering past, pickin' other words up on their backs as they go.

'I met God,' and from down the side of the sofa, he produces a little blue Bible, 'and Jesus. Jesus too.'

I sit there tryin' to assess whether he's gone a bit mental again.

'Yes. So that's the news. I'm Christian.'

Anj smiles.

'What d'you mean, "I'm Christian"?' I ask.

'Well, you're not one when you're born. You become one. If he chooses you. If he chose you.'

I look at him.

'I know it's a lot to take in. I mean, re-birth, it's like, big.'

By now, Gwen has lost all interest and is heading back towards the fish tank. At this present moment in time, I would do *anything* to be able to clamber into that tank and swim about. Anything so as to avoid this *bloody* conversation. And then I remember. Swimming lessons! I've got to sort Gwen's swimming lessons for next term.

I've drifted off, but Gareth still seems to want to discuss God and Jesus. I look at him. My brother. My brother, who's always had all this energy and anger inside him. It's not that I don't understand what he's on about. Anyone with half a brain have thought about these things. I mean, I pray and stuff. In bed. On the bus. The problem is the way he makes it sound as if he was nothing before it all happened. And he's made it sound so bloody exclusive, too. Like a club I could never get into.

'So, *I'm* not a Christian then, am I?' Gwen is blowing against the glass, drawing squiggles in the steam. She's even lost interest in the fish by now.

'Well. Who am I to say?' Gareth purses his lips. 'Maybe he's chosen you too.'

'I can't see how some people are bad people and some people are good.'

Anj pipes up. 'We're all sinners, Sam. If you don't commit your life to Jesus, then …'

Gwen is lying flat on her back on the carpet by now. Playin' dead.

'But what if you're never chosen? It's a bit like the lottery, is it? Just the luck of the draw?'

Gareth looks confused by the way my mind works. I don't reckon he's bargained for this pre-pizza discussion. I reckon he just wanted to make the announcement.

'Look,' I say in the end. Seeing that this is going nowhere fast. 'I'm glad for you, alright? I am. Personally, I've always been of the opinion that this whole business is too big to be figured out. I don't think we've got brains big enough to understand. But if you've managed to figure it out, then that's good.'

Gareth fixes me with an intense stare. I know him well enough to know that I've unnerved him. Why couldn't I just have shut my big gob? I mean, I can see why this is what he's gone for. Ever since he's come back from Iraq, he's been searchin' for something solid. Something to guide him. Something to help him make sense of things that don't seem to make much sense at all. It may as well be God and Jesus that he've found. There's much worse things he could be doin'. He could have joined a cult or started singing in a boy band, or even both at the same time.

Anj gets up. 'Better check on the pizzas.'

'You might want to put them on the top shelf for a bit.' Gareth says quietly, still looking at me.

As soon as Anj is out of the room, Gwen's up like a bolt.

'Can I sing "Pwy wnaeth …" to Uncle Gareth?'

''Course you can. Come on.'

She's a bit slow to start. Out of tune even. But after a while she gets into the flow.

> 'Pwy wnaeth y sêr uwchben?
> Y sêr uwchben, y sêr uwchben.
> Pwy wnaeth y sêr uwchben?
> Ein harglwydd Dduw!'

I'm doing the fishy sign with my hands when Anj comes in with two plates of pizza. One with chicken and spinach. And one with a smattering of tomato puree.

> 'Pwy wnaeth y pysgod chwim?
> Y pysgod chwim, y pysgod chwim?
> Pwy wnaeth y pysgod chwim?
> Ein harglwydd Dduw!'

'That's sweet!' Anj interrupts. Looks at Gareth. 'What's she sayin'?'

Gareth closes one eye, tries to remember his Welsh. Gwen just stands there.

'It's "Who made the stars above?"' I pipe up, 'An' the fish, everything in the world. God. God made 'em.'

Anj smiles. 'From school, is it?'

'Nope. I taught her that one.'

'Can I sing another song, Mam?' As per usual, Gwen is beginning to enjoy the limelight.

Only I know it's time to stop now. Eat pizza.

'After, is it? Come by here and have some of this pizza first.'

Within a few minutes, we're all chompin' away in silence. Glad of the quiet, and glad that all our personal beliefs have been stuffed back into our own heads. Only thing is, we all know they're still there. In the silence. Swimming about. Like fish in a tank.

♥

Little Gwen is sitting on the sofa, her feet in a basin of warm water. It's a treat I let her have sometimes, just before going to bed. It's Mam who started it, over her house one summer, after they'd been pottering in the garden. She's munching on a piece of toast and jam 'cos she didn't manage to eat much of the pizza over Gareth's.

I stroke her forehead, pull her fringe back, and look at the blond streaks in her hair. Her buttery-soft hair.

'Mam make a phone call now,' I say, dialling, 'about ewer swimming lessons.'

'Can I have stori Cymraeg after? The one you keep in your head, about Siencyn y gwair?'

But the phone's ringing, so I just nod to keep her quiet. Her feet swish around in the warm water.

'Noswaith dda, good evenin', Leisure Centre.'

'Noswaith dda,' I answer back. Gwen is all eyes, looking up at me admiringly.

'Sorry love, I don't speak Welsh, I just know the greetin'. What can I do for you? This line's closin' in a bit.'

'Swimmin' lessons it is, for my daughter,' and I smile

at Gwen, licking my thumb and wiping off some jam she has on her chin.

'You've left it a bit late, love. For January, is it?'

'Aye, yeah, after Christmas. I heard there's Welsh lessons startin'.'

'Ummh,' the girl hesitates. 'Let me just check with the manager by 'ere,' and then her hand goes over the receiver and I can hear a muffled conversation. Then a pause.

Gwen kicks her feet around in the water. I give her a look to stop, only she laughs. Does it again.

Soon the woman comes back on the phone, 'Hello?'

'Hyia,' I say, holdin' Gwen's legs in place.

'I'm afraid we haven't had enough names,' the girl says, trying to fake disappointment. I'm not that bothered about it really, I just want her to have swimmin' lessons.

'Oh, okay then, have you got English ones?'

'Of course we have, yeah. Is she a beginner?'

'She can't swim, if that's what you're asking.'

'Aye, there we are then, that shouldn't be a problem.'

'So those Welsh lessons,' I ask again, just to make sure I haven't confused things, in case everyone in her class is goin' to have them except her. 'You said they were supposed to be on, but they're not now, is that what ewer sayin'?'

'Well, we needed twenty children, see. And there's only seventeen on the list with ewer kid.'

'Oh, right. And you don't think it's worth me asking some of the other Mams? I'm sure I could get three more.'

'No,' the girl says, as if she's lookin' at the manager as she's speakin' to me, 'we won't be offerin' any lessons in Welsh now. Closin' date is tomorrow.'

'And you can't do it with seventeen?'

'No, love. Now, d'you want to register ewer kid? We're closin' in two.'

'Um, I might have to call back tomorrow, if that's alright.'

''Course. 'Night now,' and she puts the phone down before I even get a chance to say nos da.

Sometimes, this country gets on my nerves, I tell you. The things you can and can't do, it doesn't make sense to me. I mean, last week when we were in Caerphilly with the kids, me and Arse, we went into this little café. I wanted a cheese and ham toastie but they said they couldn't do it. There was a cheese and ham sandwich on the menu, and toast, but they said they couldn't make me a cheese and ham toastie. I swear things are the wrong way round.

Gwen pulls her feet up from the basin. Places them, pruned and warm, onto the faded pink towel I've laid out for her on the sofa.

'Right then young lady. Time for bed.'

'Nooo,' she protests. 'I not tired. I want stori Siencyn y gwair.'

'Not tonight.'

She's too tired to be angry, so she cries and clings to me, making me realise just how much she needs me. She yawns then, so I'm given permission to carry her to bed.

As I head back for the sofa, my phone rings. It's that-man-Terry.

'Only to tell you love, ewer Mam's not taken very well to this idea that Gareth's gone religious.'

'She there?'

'She've gone up early. Got one of her heads.'

'Alright. I'll pop over tomorrow. Nos da,' and I put down the phone.

I'm not mad with him for gettin' in touch, it's just I don't want to sit around and talk about it for hours. I knew Mam would be like this about it all. She's always been the one to sort Gareth's shit out. All these dramatic choices he've always made. Time and time again.

It must get really borin' after a while. Watchin' patterns develop in the same way, over and over like that. I guess when you're a parent you must see it as clear as day. 'Cos don't get me wrong, becomin' Christian might be marvellous for most people. Only it's different with Gareth. It's just not that straightforward.

Flickin' through the channels, I think about my big brother. How I had a feelin', deep down, that somethin' else was bound to come around the corner sooner or later. There's no way he could just run a bakery. Be run of the mill. It's just not him. And when these things finally emerge, you always remember, somehow, that there's only so long you can hide an ice cube.

TEASE ME

It's mornin'. Blue sky. Crisp. There are no leaves on the trees outside the old people's home, and everythin' seems tidy. Organised. Gwen's in school. Bundled in, uniform on, learnin' things. Tight blond ponytail pullin' her eyes back. Opening them up ready for the facts. Peg, on the other hand, is havin' none of it this mornin'.

'It'll be Christmas, soon,' she says, starin' at *This Morning.*

'I know. Mental. Hopefully you'll be comin' down ours.'

'Depends if I'm here.'

I give her a look. Hate the fact that she's discussin' her own death so matter-of-factly. I notice that she's dressed quite skimpily for this time of year.

'Don't you think you should pop a cardi on, Peg? That vest's awful nice, but…'

'Are you nuts? It's fuckin' well boilin' in here. They put the heatin' on full blast. I can't hack it.'

I sit back. Watch telly with her.

'Magician came yesterday.'

'Was he good?'

'Bloody diabolical.' At this, she flicks the switch and turns off the telly.

'Little Gwen doin' alright?'

'Yeah. She've asked if she can come in and see you.'

Peg ignores my comment. Looks out at the big blue sky. I notice her garishly green eyeshadow.

'Why've you turned the telly off? You love Eamonn Holmes.'

'He's gone too fat for me. Can't see the shape of his face no more.' She's quiet for a moment and then she turns to look at me. 'There's something I got to tell you...'

Before I get a chance to ask her any questions, she's up on her feet, beckoning me to come with her. In spite of myself, I follow her out into the corridor. She's so short, I can see everythin' in front of me. After a few moments, she stops by a large door that leads into the kitchen. 'Come by 'ere a minute.'

I edge closer, her see-through shoulder skin shinin' in the unnaturally bright corridor light. Leaning forward, she pushes the kitchen door open ever so slightly and peers inside.

'See him by there?' she whispers, staring over towards a young man who seems to be peeling some kind of vegetable on the stainless steel worktop. 'I'm *seein'* him.' There's a satisfied gloat in her voice. All thick and custardy from the back of her throat.

'Yeah. I'm seein' him too.'

Peg gives me a look. Rolls her eyes.

'The sex is amazin'.' I just stand there. Don't say a thing.

'Arthur, he's called. Thirty-three he is.'

'Old enough to be ewer ...'

'... My boyfriend. Yes, he is. Only we're not official yet.'

'I'm not surprised. They must have rules about things like that in here.' Her face drops then. I've obviously just touched a nerve.

'There is talk in 'ere. I can't deny it. People can feel the electricity between us, see. But if we were caught, we'd be in deep, deep shit.'

'Stop havin' me on, mun,' I look into her clear blue eyes. Eyes that look as if they couldn't tell anything but the truth.

Excitement over, we head for her bedroom.

'I know you think I've gone a step too far with this Arthur. But life's too short, love. You've got to live it.' I help her onto the bed and sit next to her. Watch her take a few tablets. If only I could lie in bed now, forget about my shift up the café.

'One more thing. I was wondering if you could do me a favour.'

I try to smile sweetly, but the problem is, you never know what kind of favour it could be with Peg. As fast as you can say paracetamol, she's produced a copy of the *South Wales Echo* from under the bed.

'I was goin' through the magazine basket in the social room the day before, lookin' for some sudoku when I found this. Six months old it is now.' I wasn't really sure where she was goin' with this to be frank.

'Anyway, I had a quick look at it, started readin' the obits and that's when I noticed a very good friend of mine had passed away. A guy who used to run this little bookstall down Ponty market. Couldn't believe I didn't know he was dead, bein' as I knew him so well at one spell. But that's how random life gets when you get to my age, see. Harry Pugh he's called. Was called.' She pauses then, as if sayin' his name out loud has brought back memories.

'I want you to take him flowers. Up Glyntaf crem.'

'Alright.' She hands me the paper.

'Give you money for the flowers next time I see you.' Only we both know full well she's never gonna pay me back. It's just the way she is.

I study her for a moment. Her small frame on top of this big bed. Her little cream vest. Her speckled neck. Her jet black hair. All that life inside such a tiny little body. By the time I look at her face again, my little terrier of an aunty is sound asleep.

I think about leaving a note for her to say that I've gone, but then I decide not to bother. After all, what's the point of writing down the bleedin' obvious?

I head for work, studyin' the obituary.

H. Pugh
Died peacefully on 14th November.
Loving parent and spouse.
Until we meet again.

BYE BYE

Crematoriums, cemeteries, remembrance gardens. They're all really weird places. If everyone in these places came back alive, they'd be teeming with life. Bloody well teeming. But that's not gonna happen today. Today, it's as dead a place as a place can be.

The birds are singing, mind. And it's a white sky day. Not going to rain. Not going to snow. Just a plain white sky for me to paint the day onto.

I look at the flowers in my hand. Red carnations. Only things they had in the garage on the way here and, truth be told, just about the only thing I could afford. Not that it matters much. Carnations or tulips. It's not as if a dead guy's gonna know, is it?

I walk towards the big wall that you can't avoid. The wall with thousands of plaques on it. Shiny and gold. Worn and silver. Fresh and old. All staring at me, begging for attention. I was here, don't you know! And I was here too! I can't help but wonder where mine will be some day, and whether they will have needed to grow another wall. I also wonder why these people haven't got gravestones. Why they decided to be plaques. It must be a decision you have to make. Or a decision somebody makes on your behalf. Says a lot about your personality I think, if you decide to be a plaque.

I search for his name for a while, until my eyes are

burning. All these names. All these souls. Gathered together even though they didn't know each other from Adam. Imagine, I think to myself as I pass a Carrie P. Donald, Gruffydd Powell, G. M. Iorwerth, L. Jones. Imagine being a plaque next to these people. I mean, I wonder whether they ever passed each other in Poundstretcher. Or had a friend in common. Or a dentist. Or a lover …

That's when I catch a glimpse of a Pugh on a plaque.

H. Pugh.

It's him. His name engraved on a shiny silver plaque. This guy who meant so much to Peg, but nothing to me.

I notice that an old woman has appeared a few feet away from me. Leaving her own flowers. For someone else I'll never get to know about either.

Just then, my phone beeps. Seems ever so inappropriate somehow. In a memorial garden.

> *Richard – Hope you're ok. Got Gwen a birthday present.*
> *Abi – Put James down for the Welsh swim lessens to. Cheers x*

Abi's spellin' really stands out in a place like this. Where all these names have been carved so carefully. So meticulously. In a funny way, it makes her seem even more alive.

And it's then that I notice a pair of brown leather shoes next to mine. Laces running down the side of the

65

leather, like weeping willow branches. I turn and catch a glimpse of an old man. He looks away. I do the same. Like a dance.

'My aunty wanted me to bring her old mate some flowers,' I point towards Harry Pugh's plaque.

'Really? That's my wife.'

I gulp as I realise that I've fucked up. Try to fish my words back into my mouth. Only it's too late. They're swimming around in the white sky now. Getting bigger. Bulging. Feeding off the embarrassment.

'Sorry. I must have got the wrong plaque,' I say then. 'Her mate was a man. Harry.'

His eyes flash for a moment. 'I'm Harry.'

My head spins as I look at him.

'Peg, my aunty is.'

He fixes his gaze on me then. 'Peg,' he says in amazement, 'how is she?'

'She's in a Home, but she's fine. Same as she always was.'

For a moment, we become aware of the fact that we are looking at each other. Weird, that. How you can be looking at someone for hours on end but then you suddenly become aware of the fact that you're looking. Which means you have to stop.

'Could you give me her address?'

I nod. Reach into my back pocket. The only paper I can find is an old receipt.

'You got a biro?'

He shakes his head, so I fumble in my coat pocket for

eyeliner pencil. I scribble down the name of the Home and pass it to him. I look at my flowers. Feel a bit pathetic.

'D'you want these?'

He shakes his head and stuffs his hands into his navy blue coat pocket. Coated leather it looks like. The kind of material that would let rain and tears slide off it.

'She'll be chuffed you're still alive,' and I smile, aware at the same time that he's here visiting his dead wife.

'Right. Best be off, then,' I say, after an awkward pause.

'Yes. Bye now,' and he turns away from me.

As I walk away, I'm sure I hear some kind of radio signal. High-pitched and weird. I don't know where the hell it's coming from so I'm forced to turn around. And that's where he is. Harry. Trying to adjust his hearing aid as it continues to go beserk.

Still embarrassed, I head off, plaques flickering their silvers and golds as I pass. There's something smug about these plaques, I think to myself. They seem to be looking down on me. An annoyingly perfect audience. They've lived their lives and forgotten their regrets. They can't make no more mistakes. Unlike me.

It's while I'm on the bus that I get the message; Mam's voice hitting my ears like freezing cold water.

'Listen love, I don't want you gettin' all worked up. But something have happened to Peg.'

♥

I pick Gwen up from school and head straight for Mam's. I'm worried sick about Peg, only I don't say anything, I

67

just listen to Gwen complaining about this *horror* in her classroom called Calypso Williams.

'... And she said to Calypso that I don't want to be friends with her no more, but I didn't say that. I wanna be friends with her. But Nia said she'd tell Miss Llewelyn and then everyone said, "Om, I'm tellin' on you." And it wasn't me who even done it.'

'Let's see if Bampy Terry's got any of those Wagon Wheels, is it?' She darts along the path and in through the front door, having forgotten everything about the previous conversation. I like the fact that she knows that the front door is open. I like the fact that she's just running in. Some day I'll have a house with a path like this. A house on the floor. With a kitchen, and a garden and a tumble dryer.

I walk straight into the lounge and come face to face with Mam, who looks worried sick.

'What's happened?'

I take off my woollen gloves, push them into my pocket. Suddenly, I spot another person sitting on the big leather chair behind her. As if he's just appeared out of thin air.

'PC Charles wants to have a word with us.'

'Alright, love?' I spot his moustache first. Then the fact that he's bald.

'Shall I make us all a cup of tea? Kettle's boiled.'

'Coffee for me, please, Mrs Jones. Three and a half sugars and a dribble of milk. Is it skimmed milk you've got?'

'Semi, sir,' Mam's gone all formal about the milk.

'Oh, then I won't have milk, then. Watchin' the figure, see.' I want to shout 'THREE AND A HALF FUCKIN' SUGARS!' in his face, but I just nod as if I understand.

Gwen pops her head around the corner. 'Terry says, am I allowed to have a Wagon Wheel before tea?' Gwen becomes shy as she notices the strange man in the front room. Mam grabs her blond ponytail, and tugs it. 'Who's a grown-up girl in ewer uniform then?'

'Aye, go on then,' I answer her finally, 'but no Skittles like last time,' and she disappears to her treat.

I sit up and look at Mr Plod.

'Can you just tell me what's goin' on?'

'Of course, Samantha. Hope you don't mind me callin' you Samantha. When Caroline, the nurse who was lookin' after Peg went in to fetch her about three, she wasn't there. And it was after that that we discovered that Arthur Rendell, one of the guys from the kitchen, had done a runner too.'

My stomach tightens and Mam returns with the coffees. PC Charles grabs hold of the steaming mug.

'Too kind, Mrs Jones, too kind.' Mam comes to sit by me. I hate how police officers can switch back and forth between makin' idle chit-chat about the tea and tellin' me whether or not my old Aunty is dead or alive, kidnapped or kidnappin'.

'So, just to get things straight. You think Peg have been kidnapped?'

Moustache-face turns to look at me again, police face on this time.

'We're just trying to establish the basic facts at the moment. Build a picture. Your aunty's gone. Mr Rendell has gone. Only there's one more thing. This Mr Rendell seems to have taken his fair share of things with him at the same time.'

My eyes pop out like golf balls. 'What? Like a robbery?'

'He took the company car. With Greenfield Homes written on the bonnet. And it seems he's taken two and a half grand from the safe too.'

I sit there, taking it all in. A lump in my throat the size of Merthyr.

'Now, I mean, both things aren't necessarily connected. Your Peg disappearin' and this man and his robbery … But it is a coincidence. And we are treating them all as one case at the moment.'

I gaze at his moustache. Wonder whether it will just wander off his face like a little gerbil one day.

'Have you ever heard her talk about this Arthur?' Moustache-face probes me further until I begin to feel like I'm on *The Bill*.

My mind is racing now. Was Peg tellin' the truth the whole time? What would she want me to say?

'Can me and Bampy Terry go down the park?' Gwen reappears, Wagon Wheel wrapper stuffed in her pink coat pocket.

'Alright. But only for a bit.'

Gwen gives Mr Moustache a suspicious look. I clock Terry by the door. Notice that he seems to be getting fatter by the day because of Mam's cakes. She's a feeder. Only in Wales you don't call it that. You call it love. 'Cos everyone does it.

'Don't let her go on the merry-go-round,' I say. 'And do her zip up.' He salutes an 'Okay, captain' and makes me cringe. And then they disappear.

Mam is in a world of her own. Thinking about Peg. 'They're supposed to be looked after. Cared for. You put them there to be cared for.'

'I never wanted her *put* there in the first place,' only Mam can't snap out of her trance.

'I mean, it doesn't make sense. Why would this Arthur take Peg with him too? If he wanted a clean get away it was hardly goin' to help to have an old age pensioner in tow.'

Just then my phone starts ringing. It's the leisure centre. I head for the kitchen to answer it.

'How are the numbers lookin'?'

'The manager is a bit concerned because we're still two kids short.'

'Right.'

'Which means we probably won't be able to hold the lessons.'

'There's still eighteen of them.'

She sighs. Doesn't like the fact that I've piped up. 'At the end of the day, they'll still be able to swim if they have their lessons in English.'

'If that's the case, why did you bother offerin' to put them on in the first place?'

'We had a request. From a Mr Arwyn Pritchard from Pen-pridd school. And we have tried, but then, sometimes these things aren't practical.'

The woman makes her excuses and ends the call. And that's when I notice that a text has come through for me while I was on the phone.

Arthur and me have done a runner. Don't tell no one I've texted. Arthur's typin, I'm dictatin. Over and out xxx p.s – check ewer hotmail.

And there it is. In boxy black letters. She's only gone and done a runner. With Arthur Rendell. I venture back towards the lounge. Stand in the doorway, feelin' like an accomplice.

'I got to go to get my daughter.'

'Of course,' Moustache-chops nods, 'we'll keep you informed.' Mam nods in acknowledgement, as if she's one of the nuns in *The Sound of Music*.

I head for the park in the twilight. Pass a few teenagers, hangin' out on a green bench under the streetlight. Harmless, they are. Only very, *very* bored-lookin'.

And then I spot them. On the see-saw. Terry sittin' on one end and Gwen on the other. Got her pink coat zipped up to her chin. Like it should be in this cold. Laughin' she is, as she goes up and down. Screamin' laughin'. Every now and then Terry makes her jump a bit with a jerky see-saw manoeuvre. Only he never takes his feet off the ground. I notice that. I watch her as she throws her head back and laughs again, her blond hair shinin' in the floodlight. I love her. Fat with the future. All that energy. All that laughter in a shitty park like this. I mean, you can hardly even call it a park anymore. Most of the swings are long gone. The merry-go-round's not working either. It's lying at an angle, facing the stars. Only that see-saw. That bloody see-saw's working a treat.

Where are you, Peg Jones? I think to myself, as I catch sight of the moon again. And what on earth are you doin'?

Hunk

'Mr Pritchard says we got to look like the real thing.'

I look at the letter again. This Mr Arwyn Pritchard has got a lot of opinions, I tell you. Okay, so he's the deputy head, but bloody hell, give me strength!

The Sioe Nadolig has got a nautical theme this year, it says in the letter. It's all about how all the fish under the sea celebrate Christmas. And this one by here has got to be dressed as a fish.

''Ave ew started ymarfer yet, then?'

'Yeah, we did do it after cinio today.'

'You *did* it. Not, you did *do* it.' She's windin' bits of her hair around her finger now and has started sucking her thumb. I start fishin' for facts.

'And is there a baby Jesus in his concert under the sea?'

'No, because it's about fish.'

'No, but, is it like the story about the little baby and the star, but under the sea?'

'There's a starfish,' she says, looking at me as if I'm dull.

'And have you got three wise men? Comin' from another sea?'

'No. But we have got this mermaid who comes to tell us that the prawns have lost their clothes in a fire and how they need our help.'

She rambles on and I'm wondering whether Mr Pritchard has been watchin' too much *Love Actually*.

'Don't worry, Mam,' Gwen adds, tryin' to calm me down as if she's a seventy-year-old woman, 'at the end of the day, it's gonna be really good.'

I'm glad that she seems happy about it, and I've got everythin' crossed that it's better than *Mamma Nia!* last year. That was quite possibly the worst version of *Mamma Mia!* I've ever seen. Worse than Pierce Brosnan's singin', even.

Next mornin' when I take her into school, I go straight to see this Mr Pritchard. I need to tell him about the swimmin' lessons and I need to ask him what he means by a fish costume too. He looks kind of cool if I remember right. A bit young to be a deputy head.

I knock on the staff room door and a young woman answers.

'Ydy Mr Pritchard yma?'

She looks at me, a little annoyed that I've even asked her a question. She heads back inside and after a few seconds, Mr Pritchard appears. Looks a bit flustered.

'Hello. Gwen's Mam, isn't it?'

Oh, shit, I think to myself. Am I gonna say I can speak Welsh? I mean, 'cos it's not as if I speak proper Welsh or nothin'. I haven't spoken it proper since school. Not really. It's bound to come out all funny.

'Ummh ... hyia. Alright? It's about these Welsh swimmin' lessons up the leisure centre ...'

And instantly, he softens. It's as if his face changes

shape. Hellish funny how some things just make people look alive all of a sudden. I notice his hair. His hair is too cool for school. Like a surfer dude from down Pembrokeshire he is. Looks as if he should be down the seashore. With the seashells.

'Have enough people come forward then, have they?'

'Well, it's like this, it is ...' and I start explaining the whole situation. He obviously shares my frustration and watches me like a hawk. Fixes his gaze.

'Right,' he says after a while. 'Well, this is not on.' He brushes his hair back and thinks. 'Look, we've got a cyfarfod staff ar ôl ysgol. Sorry.'

'Yeah, yeah. I understand.'

'O, ti'n siarad Cymraeg?' and now it's as if another see-through curtain has fallen off his eyes.

'Tipyn bach. Went to Welsh school, like, but that's ages ago now.'

He smiles, and then clicks into teacher mode again, 'Yes, so, wel, yn y cyfarfod staff heno, 'na i godi'r mater ar gyfer y minutes. See what they say. We'll sort this out.'

He's obviously a kind man, I think to myself, because he didn't want to use all Welsh sentences that would scare me off. Then soon enough, he says he has to head off. Get the Year Six kids to class. I just stand there for a moment. Sort of still smelling him. Eventually, I manage to pull myself together. Float across the yard towards the front gate.

As the bell chimes, jumpers, ties, arms and legs dart

past me in the other direction. Only I'm not really aware of anything. I'm just stuck. In the memory of him.

♥

welsh-dragon@hotmail.com. I type it in slowly and wait for the computer to kick into action.

As I wait, I look around the room. All these randoms. Sitting together. Desperate for wi-fi. Not knowing each other from Adam. I reckon the library is always full of freaks. My good self included, of course. And that's when I see it. A message. From her.

> *Sam,*
> *Darlin', you must be worried sick with it all, and I'm sorry. But I had to break free, like Freddy Mercury said doin' the hooverin'. 'Cos the thing is see, love, I've tasted the fruits of true love again. All soft, and ripe and drippy. And I'll not hold back, because I can't deny it – I've fallen hoof, line and stinker for this Arthur. Bang. Like a knock on the head. And once I realised, I just had to follow my heart. Had to, d'you hear me! We just had to be together.*

I take my eyes from the screen for a moment. Try to digest what she's saying. Only I end up looking at someone else's screen by accident. She don't look best pleased, so I turn my head.

> *We got off the ferry in France this mornin, love. (Yeah, we took the money. But what can I say?) For*

your info, the company car's in Calais. We left it there, so no one could follow our scent. To be fair on Arthur by here, the robbery was more my idea. 'Cos I'd been thinking, see. If the Home is my home, then technically I should have the right to drive the company car. Now the money, I can't actually justify, but what the hell, they'll just have to spend less on shit clowns and weird magicians from now on, won't they? And let's face it, those bastard entertainment companies only ended up leavin' us all craving for death anyway. DEATH I tell ew. (Do you know how much those bastards charge?)

Anyway, here I am, here we are. We're in Paris! Gay Paris! This place, love, you would fall over with how beautiful it all is. We've been to the Pigalle (it's like this red light sort of district). And we're planning to go to the Louvre tomorrow. (Arthur said he's gonna talk to the people in there to see if I can get a wheelchair.) All this walkin' gets a bit tirin' after a while. But by God, are we havin' a good time.

Bought a little model of the Eiffel Tower for you and little Gwen too. Must go. There's a big fat man with a beard behind me, and to be fair, we have been on this thing for ages looking for hostels.
Love to everyone at home (but obviously you can't tell them that, or they'll know you know I'm here. Oh, God!).

peg and aRHTUR XXXX

I immediately e-mail back.

Peg,

Just take care of yourself, do you hear me? And also. I've got massive news. I'm not going to go into details by here now, but Harry Pugh is still alive! I went down the cemetery, and it's his wife who's died Peg. Which means you can meet again. So come back isit? To see him?

Sam XXX

As I send the message, I notice that there's a fat man standing behind me waiting to go on the internet too. Only this bloke hasn't got a beard. And I'm not looking for hostels in Paris. I'm sittin' in a library in Ponty, gutted that I have to go to work.

From where I'm sitting I notice that it's just started peltin' it down outside. Fan-bloody-tastic I think to myself, smiling at the fat man as I get up from my seat. Soakin' wet trousers and a gob-full of rain as I wait for the bus. Nothin' better.

♥

I'm all sticky with sweat by the time I get to the café, the idea of a five-hour-long shift filling me with dread. And that's when I see him. As clear as day. Sitting on his own drinking black coffee.

To begin with, I can't even work out how he's found me. How he's tracked me down in the café. But as soon as I'm sat with him, it begins to make sense. He says he's been up the Home. Which means he knows everything – well, nearly. I look at him. His eyes full of this new story.

'I just really hope she's safe,' he says after a long silence. 'The police must have some idea where this brute has taken her.'

I daren't tell him that I just e-mailed her saying that he's still alive. I daren't even think it in case it shows in my eyes.

'Listen,' I say, feeling the invisible rope of Pauline's eyes dragging me back towards the counter. 'I can't chat now. I'm in work.'

'Then visit me,' he says. 'We'll go for a coffee in Rhiwbina. That's where I live now.'

'I want to help,' he says then, and I smile a grateful smile before heading for the counter. By the time I get there, he's gone. This man I don't really know from Adam.

'Didn't know you were into the older man,' Carol says, laughing at her own joke before she's even finished delivering it. I smile a sarcastic smile and head for the kitchen. Intent on washing away this whole damn mess with the suds.

MEET ME

So the weird thing is, when I meet him, he doesn't look best pleased to see me. Now, correct me if I'm wrong, but the argument would be that he was the one who invited me here in the first place. And I mean, it took me absolutely ages to get down here. Train from Ponty to Cardiff Central. Bus from the middle of Cardiff to Rhiwbina. I wonder whether he realises I haven't got a car.

A waiter with black trousers comes over with this posh tea. In a teapot it is, this tea. A see-through teapot like as if we're living in the future. Harry says he thinks I'll like it but I'm not really so sure I can trust his taste in tea. I mean I'm used to Tetley's for starters, but on top of that, he's got this weird beret thing on his head today. Never trust a man with a weird hat on his head – I'm sure I've heard that sayin' someplace before.

'So,' he says after a while, lifting the teapot lid, giving the golden tea leaves a stir with a shiny silver spoon from a fairytale. I watch the leaves spin in the water. It looks a bit like the snow dome thing I used to keep next to my bed when I was little. Only that this is tea. In a teapot.

'Yeah,' I say then, looking at the cup and saucer the waitress has put in front of me. Some words just come out. They're not meant for anything except to cushion the blow of emptiness and awkwardness.

I wait for Harry to pour the tea with his shaky hands. Only in the end I'm so shit scared it's gonna go all over him, I help him. I study his face as we pour the tea. The annoying sound of running water makin' my shoulders tense up.

As soon as I've sipped the tea I know it's not for me. It's bitter and watery.

'What's the latest? With Peg.'

I shake my head as if to say there isn't any news.

'I saw the item on *Wales Today.*'

Harry lowers his eyes now. Stirs his tea with shaky, determined hands. Just then I hear that familiar mechanical squeak. His hearing aid. Playin' up again. Like an unruly mouse he keeps in his ear. He reaches for it. Twiddles and fiddles as if it's second nature before reaching for his cup of tea and taking a careful sip. I watch him as he looks down at the saucer, landing his cup back onto the porcelain circle with the precision of a pilot landing a plane on a runway.

Just then, I have a sudden urge to tell him the truth about Peg only, thankfully, I manage to hold back. After all, I hardly know this guy. Why would I risk telling him something so huge? Maybe he'd go straight to the police. Put me and Peg in the shit. Before you know it, Interpol would be involved and Peg and Arthur would be whisked back to Wales, leaving half-sipped Cosmopolitans on a table somewhere.

'How did you two know each other? Just from the market?'

Harry nods.

'I had a little stall there. Books. Some of my art.'

'Artist, are you?'

'Well. Yes, I suppose I am.'

'And what? You just got to talkin'?'

'You know what Peg's like. It only took her five minutes. Used to come down when Alf was down the pit. Swallowed books she did. Especially those ridiculous love stories based in places like Greece or India. Loved them.'

I study him then. Try to understand how they would have formed such a bond over a few poxy books. Only I daren't pry. It doesn't seem right somehow. Not today, at least.

I sip my tea. An awkward silence spreading like black ink over the white tablecloth. Inching closer with every second. Creeping towards me like deltas in the white cotton.

Desperate, I decide to immerse myself in the lives of others who are in this café. People enjoying a nice, simple afternoon. A mother feeding her son with tight little black curls on his head. Two friends hiding shopping bags under their chairs. Sharing the same menu. A breezy-looking waitress with very small ears picking up a fork that's fallen to the floor. How clean and tidy her world seems. How lucky she is to have such a lovely shaped chin.

'Right then,' says Harry, finality permeating his voice, 'lets take a walk.'

He holds his hand up and the waitress instinctively turns and glances at it. He mouths 'the bill', without making a sound, and smiles at her. Like a dance, I think. Like a dance in France or somewhere. I get to the counter just as he's tossing a few shiny fifty pence pieces into the white ceramic tip bowl by the till. Fat lot of good a bowl like that would be up the caff. You have to have customers for that type of thing to work.

♥

Having tea was a bad idea. When you have tea, you have to face someone. Gesture. Check out body language. But in a car, in a car, it's alright. And on walks too. Because words just come out. And you don't have to worry about staring someone else in the face. Us humans are a funny bunch, aye.

'Let's go in here,' he says, and we glide towards a gallery next door to a charity shop.

I can't say I've ever been into an art gallery before, and so I take extra care that I don't trip over my own feet. I imagine myself slamming into a painting and taking the walls down with me. All quite realistic considering the experiences I've had of late.

'What d'you think about this piece?' he asks after a little walk past a few paintings. I glance at the picture in front of me. Start at the corners and work myself towards the middle. I haven't got the faintest idea how you're supposed to look at a painting. People don't teach you this stuff, least they didn't in our school anyway.

'It's a forest, is it? I can't make it out.'

'Do you like it?' he asks and I get fuzzy with it. Shades of green, diagonal brush strokes and bark too. Brown bark. And then a slice of crimson and orange flooding through the whole thing. The sun, I think it's supposed to be. Yeah, that's what it is. The sun. Its light spilling through the branches on a cold winter's day.

'Makes me think about morning thoughts. Good paint too. Makes you want to touch it.'

He smiles and as soon as he does, I notice the initials on the painting. HP. In black ink.

'Oh my God, it's you. Nuts.'

We continue towards a park like two little squirrels and I feel winter in everything we do. December's boldness. It sort of makes things clean and complicated, as if we're living in the olden times. There are cars rushing by in every direction, but I don't even seem to hear their hum.

'I know where Peg is, by the way,' I say, looking straight ahead, 'and she's fine.'

He stops immediately. Turns his head to look at me. Only I daren't look over. I stuff my fists into my pockets for my fingers to feel about for bits and pieces to clutch onto. An old mint imperial, some tissue and an intriguing object that I can't for the life of me work out what it is. I can't believe I've told him. Only it's too late now. So I may as well carry on.

'She's done like a great escape thing. Disappeared with her boyfriend.'

'That young chap?'

I nod. He raises an eyebrow.

'I e-mailed her to say you were still alive.'

'And what did she say?'

'She haven't replied. Only I'm sure she's over the moon,' I say politely. If a little pathetically. 'I'm desperate for her to come home. We all are. And I was thinkin' maybe you could help me.'

'Why do you want her to come home?' I look at him. Wonder what's goin' on in his head.

'I wanna know that she's alright.'

'Didn't she tell you that she's fine?'

I'm a bit surprised by his reaction. Don't really know what to say.

'Peg's a free spirit, Sam,' he says then. 'Don't you think she should be able to do what she wants?'

As we walk through the deserted park, silence washes over us both again. I'm confused by his attitude. I'd have thought he'd share the same desperation to get her home and safe.

Late afternoon seems to be pulling her strings. Parents fetching children from school. Other people in their offices, dreaming about five o' clock. Carol probably having a cuppa in the caff and that-man-Terry stood outside the school gates waiting for Gwen with a Wagon Wheel in his left pocket. Late afternoon always smacks of normality. The day to day grind of things. Except our afternoon was nothing of the sort.

'You won't tell no one, will you, Harry?'

'Who have I got to tell?' He's looking straight ahead again now. Digesting the information.

December air tries to get in between my layers so I hunch my shoulders up to keep warm. Disturbed by the same wind, Harry lifts his hands up to his mouth, blows into his fist and puffs like a steam train.

'Give what I said some thought,' he says as we reach the gated entrance. 'Sometimes we push for the wrong things. That's all I'm saying.'

♥

It's when I get off the bus that I spot one. Only I soon clock more. Dotted up the road, glued onto trees and lampposts. Peg posters. Her face covering half the paper.

MISSING
Peggy Lee Jones
(also known as Peg, Pegs and Gaffer)
Have you seen this lady?
If you have, please contact the number
below

Gaffer, I think to myself. Who in the world calls her Gaffer? I swear a person can be a million different people sometimes.

Standing there looking at the poster, something seems to clash. It's something to do with seeing paper stuck to a tree. I suppose it's a bit like someone putting ketchup on a tomato.

I march towards Mam's house. Annoyed by it all.

'Mam,' Gwen says matter of factly, as she spots me coming in through the front door. 'I gorra seren aur today. For being good on the computer.'

'Da iawn!' I smile, plonking my bag by the coat rack. Gwen just marches upstairs, blasé about her achievement. I head for the lounge and clock that Gareth's here too. Mam looks up from their conversation.

'Oh, hi love. Listen, I can't sit and chat. I'm meeting the police now, got a community meeting about Peg,' and that's when I notice her T-shirt. A picture of Peg punches me in the gut. All over her boobs and her belly it is. Peg's face. Spread out so far it doesn't really look like Peg at all. I read the writing on the T-shirt.

Have you seen this lady?

Gareth spins Mam around, proud as punch. I read the back of her.

Sponsored by Bread of Heaven – your bakery

I stare at Gareth in disbelief. 'You can't be seen to be makin' money out of the fact she's missin'!'

'We've got to do something, bach,' says Mam, desperation seeping out from every pore. And I hate to say it, but for a minute I can even smell the fact that searching for Peg seems to have given her a cause. Something to fight for. Like when she had us in the house.

'Me and Anj have been prayin' too,' Gareth says, but Mam doesn't stop there. 'And they're doin' a programme on the Welsh language channel too, love.' Just saying this fills Mam's little heart up with hope. I can hear it pumping with bright red blood. 'Apparently, tons of people disappear from old people's homes every year. They reckon there's a secret economy. A black market. For pensioners. Sick, innit?'

I've tried hard to contain myself up until now. Only, knowing the truth always makes it impossible for you to act normally.

'Don't we just need to calm down a bit?'

'What do you think we should do? Sit at home and twiddle our fingers?' says Mam then.

'The producer guy who called round was interested in the fact I'd been out in Iraq, too,' Gareth says, thinking about the cash, no doubt. 'I think he wants to make a documentary. See how some of us have re-built our lives.'

Mam doesn't even look at Gareth, scared for the life of her it might bring everything back.

'You haven't spoken Welsh in years, Gar,' I say, tryin' to put him off. Only I feel dirt guilty for saying it.

'For your poxy information, it wouldn't be for S4C.' He looks over towards Mam. He's long since clocked her anxiety and knows exactly what I'm getting at. 'I told you before, Mam. It's different now. I can handle it.'

Mam doesn't move a muscle because she's thinking about her little boy. She doesn't want him to go and blow himself up again. Gareth zips up his coat in one smooth action. He can see there's no use even starting this conversation.

As Gwen and me leave for the flat, I get a massive craving for reality. Boring, relentless reality. No bullshit. No imagination. No crazy aunties travellin' the world. Just normal day to day shit like putting out the bins and making yourself a cup of tea that's not quite strong enough but will do the job.

I reckon reality's gonna make a comeback pretty soon. 'Cos it's got a lot going for it. It doesn't try to trip you up or pretend to be anything it's not. It doesn't make you dream about things that will never actually happen. It don't build up your hopes either. It just unwinds in front of you, like a long dirt-track road.

Happy Birthday

'Everyone smile!' Arse's digital camera blinds us with its over-the-top flash. Ten wild-looking little girls and me in a photo. Perry and Carly are on the floor behind Arse. The level of noise is astonishin'. It's pourin' down outside, the sky black like soot. But the lights are on in here. Serious lights.

'I'm seven as well before long,' I catch Mari and Gwen's conversation before they begin to march. The other girls soon follow until they form a little chain around the sofa. All glittering little pink gems they are, in their fairy outfits.

'D'you want one of these?' Arse asks, holding a plate of fondant fancies under my nose. But I don't really fancy anything. I've been feeling a bit peaky all day.

'Lets go and have a fag, isit?' she asks, desperate to get away from the noise.

'Reit 'te, girls, amser watcho ffilm. Yeah?' I turn to Arse. 'Perry can sit with them too, can't he?' And they all screech 'Yeah!' at a pitch that only dogs can tune into properly. Arse picks Carly up and heads towards the kitchen.

'Can Amber sit by *me*?' Gwen asks, and I nod. I don't know what that means politically in the group, I just want them to shut up, and start feelin' sleepy after all the food they've eaten. Gwen's blond hair is hidden under a pink hat she demanded to wear for the party. I've bought her this DVD for her birthday – *Disney's Greatest* – and I'm ripping the plastic off it now. I can't do it quick enough.

Soon there isn't a sound to be heard. And people wonder why us parents put kids in front of the telly. By the time I get to the kitchen, Arse has made us both a cup of tea.

'Nice telly you've got.'

'Buy as you view,' and she can't hide that look. Her and Alan can afford to buy their own telly. Whoopee for them.

'You gonna sell those pups?' Arse asks, looking down at Molly and the little ones scrambling about.

'Aye,' I say, 'put an advert in the post office day before yesterday. Why, you want one?'

'You jokin' me? No way.'

We head for the balcony with our teas. The smell of concrete that's been pelted by rainfall floods my senses.

'Ewer parents comin' over?'

'If you mean Mam and Terry, yeah. My brother's comin' too. Him and twatface.' There's a long, awkward silence. 'And no, he isn't comin'. Before you ask.' I know that's what she's getting at. I just know it. I can hear how defensive I sound, but I can't help it. 'I've told him he can come up Christmas Day with some stuff, but he's not comin' for her birthday. I wouldn't be able to hack it.'

I hate it when she does this. She's done it forever and a day. She thinks I'm not facing up to my emotions. She thinks I'm refusing to deal with things. Only she doesn't know the half of it. Not even the quarter of it.

'Any news about Peg?' she asks, trying to change the subject. I shake my head, swallowing down my fag smoke. Another brick wall that's come between us because I can't say a thing.

'Look, I know you're stressed, but they will find her, you know. They will.' I nod. Feel like shit for not sayin' anything.

'How's everything going with Alan up the council?' and she indicates a 'so-so' by pursing her lips and tilting her head.

'We should go out some night, shouldn't we?' she says, looking at Carly. 'I could do with a night off.'

I smile then, because I know deep down we'll never get round to it.

'I'm gonna go before ewer family arrives.'

'Don't be stupid, mun. Stay.'

But she shakes her head, and in a weird way, I'm glad. She's making me feel awkward with the truth of her today. She knows me so well she doesn't even have to ask the questions anymore. They just sit there, in the silence, screamin' – until I buckle under the pressure and prove her right.

MY GIRL

My Darlin,

You will not BELIEVE where I am by now? I'm only in Barcelona, Cata-bleeding-lonia! Now, I got to tell you, things haven't been goin' smoothly with me and Arthur. He wants kids and I … only kiddin' love. But I'll tell you ('cos it's bloody well nice to be able to get it off my chest to someone else), I do sometimes think that the age difference is goin' to be a bit of a barrier, you know. In terms of my needs, I mean. In terms of a way an older woman needs her lovin' (of course, we're quite open about the whole thing. I mean, he's the one doin' the typin' now, for instance. Thank God no one in this Hotel done understand Valleys English innit love! I'm dictatin' full blast by here!)

I hope ewer Mam is ok, and that little Gwen had a lovely birthday. I did think of her a few times on the day. But Barce-bloody-lona. Let me tell you my love. Let me tell ew! There's this area right, called Las Ramblas, no word of a lie, it's amazin' (that's where Arthur came out with how much he loves me), it's that kind of place, you know. It just makes you say the things that are on ewer mind. Now, granted, we're not in the heat of summer here now, but it's ever so special. We found one place just off

Las Ramblas called Plaza Del Pi. Oh my, you would have loved it. You would have. And you will, if you ever get a chance to come over.

Anyway, to cut a long story short, I'm not a religious person, as you know, but when I saw the Sagrada Familia (this massive church thing, Sam), I swear I nearly could say, there IS a God. It's the prettiest thing. All fine and spikey and bits of shiny glass winkin' in the sunlight. Ewer Nanna would 'ave gone beserk if she would have seen it. She had a thing for churches even though she was Chapel. She always tried to get ewer Gramps to take her to see different churches all over Wales. But he'd have none of it. Said they made him cold to the bone. Made his colliers' fingers white.

I got to go now. I'm starvin' and even though Arthur made the most of the all-you-can-eat brekky in the Hostel, I just couldn't. (Love, they give ew raw meat and salad and things for breakfast. I couldn't stomach it, I couldn't. Well, I mean, I can't stand salad at the best of times. But for breakfast! I mean, cold cured ham, cheese, eggs? For breakfast? What in hell's name's wrong with them?) So, see, I need dinner. And quick too. Because I've got a tendency to lose my rag if I haven't had food. Low blood sugar and all. Tapas we're gonna have. All different foods on little plates. Hope I don't get nothin' slimey.
Adios, my darlin, message you soon,
Peg and Arthurrr xxx

p.s – very surprised, I was, to hear about Harry.
Have you met him then? What did he have to say?

I type back:

Peg,
Sounds like you're havin' an amazin' time.
Obviously you're probably aware of the fact that the
police are after you and Arthur now, but I've got
you covered. The only other thing to say is that I met
Harry last week. He's a lovely man and I think he's
looking forward to you comin' back home. Only, I
know it's not goin' to be that simple now that the
police are after you.
Enjoy. Jealous.
Sam X

Leaving the library, I walk along the cold Pontypridd streets, imagining I'm wearing a flamenco dress. I may be on my way to catch a bus to a shitty café with a shitty new menu, but in my head I'm whizzin' about on Las Ramblas with a red rose behind my ear. And even though I'm completely aware of how deluded I am, I don't really care. At least not for today.

CRAZY

'Boni-jorno,' a wide smile with no meanin' beams in front of my eyes. 'What would you like?'

'Are you havin' a laugh?' I look at Carol. I've already noticed that she's wearin' white trousers and a white top with a white hat on her head like a pizza maker. But it's that red scarf I can't hack. No way am I wearin' that.

'Your uniform's in the back.'

And just then, a customer comes in. Ray it is, Ray the Betting. All creaky and old and sweet.

'Ben Ven Wto a Glanvillas!' Carol shouts, like an Italian mamma. 'What can I get you?'

Ray stares up at the new menu up above us on the wall.

'What's all this?'

'Change of menu, Ray. We are now an Italian caff.'

'Isit,' he says, without askin' a question.

Carol waits patiently as the Pavarotti CD plays the second song, probably for the third time this morning.

'I just want beans on toast.'

'Right,' says Carol, puzzling how this fits in with the new order of things, 'that means you'll have to go for the tapas.'

'Tap what?'

'You have to choose at least four things from that list

up by-there.' She points above her, and to the left, where all the tapas ingredients have been noted.

I take a look for myself. Beans. Olives. Mozzarella. Toast. Bread. Butter. SQUID!! Bacon. Eggs. Pasta. Cheddar Cheese. Lettuce. Anchovies. Spaghetti Hoops. Tomatoes. Ice-cream. Jacket Potato.

'I don't quite get it,' he scratches his head, looks a bit stressed out.

'All you have to do, Ray love, is just choose four things from up by there.'

Ray goes to fetch his glasses from his coat pocket. Fumbles around for a few seconds. Eventually, he finds them, puts them on a bit crooked and stares up at the list. Knackered.

'Well, I'll have beans … and I'll have, I'll have bread, no, sorry … toast and butter then …' He looks at Carol again, taking off his glasses, 'is that alright love?'

Carol's scribblin' down the order, 'And one more thing,' she mumbles, head down. 'You need to order one more thing.'

'Don't want anythin' else, love. That's me done.' He reaches for his wallet.

'You've got to have four,' Carol says, stubbornly. 'Or else ewer payin' for four and havin' three, see. It's the tapas rules.'

'Who is this bloody tapas anyway?' Ray fumbles for his glasses again, places them on his nose. As he looks up at the menu, I can see that his neck has gone all blotchy and red.

'What about eggs? Do you want eggs?'

'Not particularly, no.'

'Or mozzarella?'

'Mozza-what?' Ray sighs. 'Look, forget it, right?'

Carol looks up from her notes.

'I'll go home and make my own dinner. That way I can have what I want, and watch *Loose Women* at the same time.' And just like that, he disappears.

Carol just stands still for a moment. Scarily silent. Everything about her tells me she's just about to cry. I take a look around the caff and clock Boshy sittin' in the corner, munchin' on somethin' that looks a lot like a toastie. Apart from him, the whole place is empty.

'How come Boshy's got his usual toastie then? Don't see how he'd be able to get it by the "tapas rules".'

'Didn't have the 'eart to tell him, did I.'

And then she's off. Tears streamin' down her face. For a minute, she brings back memories of the woman from Lovelife.com. Only to be fair, this really isn't like Carol.

'This place is goin' to the dogs, mun.'

'Let's go for a fag, isit?'

She shakes her big head. Tears runnin' down that bit between her nose and her upper lip that goes on forever. It's like a slide, I think to myself. A slide for her fat tears.

'Fag'll do you good, mun. Who've you got to serve?'

Carol looks around. Pavarotti booming from the little CD player with dust on the top.

'Give us a shout if someone comes in will ew, Bosh?'

and Bosh does a thumbs up, bless him, although I doubt very much that he understood a word of what I was sayin'.

It's cold outside, and even though I've got a warm coat on, I'm still gettin' goosebumps. Carol, on the other hand, is standin' there in her white outfit.

'Don't ew wanna put a coat on, Car?' I ask. 'It's bloody nobblin'.'

'I don't feel the cold,' she says after a while, all distant and weird.

I take out two fags and fetch the lighter, hand one to Carol. She doesn't take it so I light 'em both myself. The orange flame brings back memories I didn't even know I had. Like a heat from another time.

'Fuck Christmas,' she says, all out of the blue.

'Aye. Fuck it.'

As Carol swallows down smoke, she begins to cough and splutter. I don't think she's ever done this in her life before. We've all got our vices mind, haven't we. Food obviously bein' hers. Annoyed by the fact that she's not making the most of her cigarette, I reach for it. Got one in each hand now. Alternate my smokin'.

'Listen. I heard about …'

''Course you did. Bad news travels faster than fuckin' bird flu, I tell you.' As she stares straight into the garden of the house in the row ahead, I think about the fact that I heard her say 'bird flew' rather than 'bird flu'. Even though it's midday, the shadows remain. And for a moment then, I'm reminded of Harry's painting.

The greens of the trees, the brown of the bark, and the shards of light slicing like glass through the woodland branches.

'The boys comin' back for Christmas Day?' I glance down at her new white shoes. Like Mam's white **Missing Peg** T-shirt. Too white for the crap we're talkin' about.

''Spect so,' she says, 'and bringin' those tarts with 'em too, no doubt. D'you know, not even one of 'em have ever taken me on a trip to nowhere. Too busy in their own little heads they are. Self-obsessed. Theresa haven't even probably got the energy. Lives on them bloody protein shakes. Stupid girl.'

I wonder whether Mam thinks that about me. That I'm just all up in my own head. Whizzin' around like a Catherine wheel.

'Where's *he* gonna be then? With his brother?'

Carol looks at me then. A look that nearly breaks my heart. Pauline doesn't seem to have given me the full story. Only now, Carol has given me the rest of it. With one look. He's only gone and buggered off with someone else. Men. I swear to God.

'Who'd wanna be stuffin' turkey with a minger like me?'

I puff on both fags at the same time for a moment, tryin' to think of what to say next.

'What's this? A W.I. meetin', isit?' Glanville's annoying voice booms at us from the back door. He looks as if he could strangle us both.

'Carol's feelin' poorly.'

Carol nods, hardly able to keep her tears from splatterin' all over the floor.

'Get in, isit?' His voice is cool now. Quiet with the power that he has over us.

As I follow him inside, I become convinced that he's lost some hair over the past few days. Then suddenly, he turns around and faces Carol and me.

'How's the Italiano comin' on?'

'Not bad,' Carol can barely muster up the energy to sound enthusiastic. It's friggin' well obvious for everyone to see that it's a complete and utter flop.

'I want things to be better than *not bad*, Carol. I'll have you know I've spent *thousands* of pounds on this makeover. I am NOT gonna sit about and let it go down the shit-hole!'

'Thing is,' I venture, 'there's already one Italian caff ...' Glanville glares at me. After a beat, he takes a step back. Pavarotti's 'Nessa Dormat' in full flow.

'You think you're smarter than everyone, don't you, Sam?'

'Do we have to do this in front of the customers?' Carol's thick lips mutter.

'What customers, Carol? There's only Bosh here. Eatin' his bloody TOASTIE.'

Carol lowers her head, ashamed that she's broken the tapas rules.

'Look,' he loosens his shirt collar, 'I'm tryin' to put my faith in you here. D'you think this is easy for me? I got two hairdressers to think about too.'

I head for the sink and start washing up. Sometimes it's the best thing you can do. Submerge yourself in suds and warm water. Forget about the world.

I'm tryin' to dry my hands with an already damp tea towel when my mobile rings.

'You better come home, love,' Mam says, quietly.

'What is it? Tell me.'

'I don't want to. Not on the phone.'

'Mam, mun. What is it?'

'It's Peg, love.'

Cool Dude

By the time I get to the house, Mam's already left for the morgue down Cardiff. Fat-man-Terry and Gwen are watching a cartoon from the 80s and my stomach's churning. I can't believe Mam has to go through this. Lifting up the blanket. Checking the body. Peeking through her splayed hand. Then I think about Peg. Lyin' on a beach. Sippin' on a cocktail. Oblivious to all this bollocks.

'Sit down, mun,' Terry doesn't take his eyes off the screen. 'It won't do your hips no good rockin' back and forth like that.'

'When's she due back, did you say?' I ask again, even though I know I only just asked a few minutes back. He looks up at me.

'No point thinking the worst until you've got to. Learned that years back when I thought my sister wasn't pulling through the chemo. Look at her now. Running every Zumba class from here to Ebbw Vale.'

I smile at him, because I know what he's getting at. And for the very first time, I kind of begin to imagine what it must feel like to be a psychopath. All those things I know that I'm not tellin'. It's as if my head is full of truth and everyone else is just play-acting.

Just then we all hear the front door. Then we hear Mam's voice, talkin' to someone. And then we see him. Fat moustache face. Enterin' the lounge with Mam. I swear his eyes look as if they're melting down over his cheeks.

I stare at Mam's face. She's obviously been crying. She's wearing a great big brown scarf too. Makes her look like a snowman. She looks over towards me then. Shakin' her head, with pain in her eyes.

'It wasn't her.'

Gwen looks up from the cartoon. All eyes.

'Go an' fetch Nanna's china dolls from upstairs, bach,' but she's reluctant. 'Go on. I'll be up now.'

Terry switches the telly to mute and Gwen does as she's told. Mam just stands there. Chewin' on the inside of her cheek.

'We've had a few sightings,' PC Charles says then. 'Bognor Regis, Llanharry and Boots in Pembroke Dock.' And I nearly want to laugh out loud because of the bollocks of it.

Mam heads over towards Terry. Sits on the sofa next to the cardboard box full of the Peg T-shirts. Terry gives her a cwtsh. All skin and shirt. I get a hunch that PC Charles seems ever so slightly jealous.

Moustache-chops coughs awkwardly.

'Right then. Best be off.'

Mam sits up.

'Thanks Malcolm, appreciate the lift back,' and the first-name-terms business hits my ears a bit funny. Fat-man-Terry doesn't flinch.

'Here,' Mam gets up and reaches into the cardboard box, 'take a T-shirt.'

She hands PC Charles a **Missing Peg** T-shirt and he smiles, grateful. As he shuts the door after himself, Gwen reappears, holding a blusher brush.

'Can I put real make-up on the dolls?'

I tell her she can't and her eyes bulge. There's nothing like asking for permission when you've actually already done something. Retrospective planning they call it up the council.

'Why you sad, Nanna?' Gwen asks Mam. And I suddenly feel a lump in my throat.

'Your Anti Peg it is, bach. We just want to make sure she's alright.' I watch as tears well up in Mam's eyes like lakes. And that's when it washes over me. Cool like water. This has got to stop. And I'm the only one who can make it happen.

♥

Next morning, I'm sitting in the posh café in Rhiwbina. Waiting for him. Mam didn't sleep a wink last night, apparently. Every time she closed her eyes, she kept thinking about the dead woman she saw down the morgue. For some reason, she went on and on about her neck on the phone. Said it was so upsetting to see it. A dead neck. No breath flowing through it.

By the time he gets here, I'm on my second cup of tea. It's runnin' through me. Like a warm river. He sits down, all out of breath and flustered. While he has his eyes on other things, I study him, as if he's a rare bird. And as soon as he seems like he's in the room, I tell him what I intend to do.

'I'm going to the police. About Peg. I've decided.'

He sits still for a moment. As if he's made from stone.

'It's gone too far now. Mam had to identify an old woman's body yesterday. 'Cos they thought it was her.'

I watch him as he puts his hands on the table. It's nearly as if they're not his.

'She'll be in a lot of trouble if you tell the authorities.'

'She's gonna be sooner or later, anyway. What d'you want. Tea?'

He nods and I call the waitress over. The one with the perfect chin.

'You know that she's bound to come home eventually,' he says, once the waitress has gone.

'I know that. And I did think about what you said. Only look at the damage she's causin'. So will you help me?'

'I can understand that it's a lot for you to deal with …'

'Not me. It doesn't bother me. I know the truth. But my Mam thinks she could be lyin' on the bottom of the Taff. D'you know what I mean?'

Harry nods. Because he does understand.

'Why don't you just send her an e-mail? Ask her for confirmation of when she's planning on coming back. At least you'll know then.'

I sit there. Feel like I've turned up a cul-de-sac of a conversation.

'I don't understand. Why you can't see it's best for her to come home?'

'Couldn't you tell your mother? That would help, wouldn't it? It doesn't matter about the police.'

I'm stopped in my tracks. I suppose it's a fair point. She's the only one that's really hurting. Well, apart from Gareth. But he's got God.

Just then, a text arrives on my phone. It's Richard. The waitress glides over and places the tea in front of Harry. I swear you pay more for the dancin' than the tea in this place. We settle down to a normal chat, and I talk a bit about the disaster that is Richard and me.

'What does he do?'

'Nothin'. He lost his job 'cos he was so obsessed with his band. But they're gonna be massive,' I say pointedly and Harry raises an eyebrow in acknowledgement.

He smiles then, and I smile back at him. Glad that anyone gives a toss. As we leave he throws a few fifty pence pieces into the white bowl again. It's like when you toss money into a fountain as a kid, I think to myself. That strange, silvery glistening. That nod to the future. Begging it to be gentle with you, because we all know how strong some winds can blow.

HEART-THROB

Sam,

*I don't 'spect you'll be able to believe me now, right,
but guess where we are now... you'll never guess!
You'll never ... We're only in Venezuela! I mean,
I'd hardly heard of the place 'til we found it on
the map! We were lyin' naked on our hostel beds
in Barca (we did 'ave a room of our own, I'll have
ew know, I haven't gone all native or nothin') and
we said we'd play a game. Arthur was gonna drag
his finger all down the place names on the back of
our little atlas and then I was supposed to say stop!
Can ew believe it?! (First place his finger landed on
was in the Outer Hebrides but we weren't gonna
go there, were we?) We played the game again and
it landed on Venezuela. Anyway, I said I wouldn't
mind if we just went there (Venezuela, I mean),
'cos I've got quite a lot of Alf's compo left and
well, if you don't spend it while ewer here isn't it
... Sayin' that, the money we took from the Home
just went like that. With a click of the fingers.*

*So, yeah, we're here. In Caracas, which is like
the capital city or somethin'. Lovely it is. All
South American. There was this leader here, until
recently. Man of the people he was. Chávez. Bit of
a hero. There's another one in now. Maduro, he's*

called. He's on the left too. Very workers together it is here. Like Wales before you was born.

There is one thing buggin' me though. The food. It's a bit weird. And the weather, well, it's quite dry but I don't know, on the whole, I suppose I must admit, I'm missin' home. Not the Home, I'll have you know. But the Rhondda, like. I just feel, it doesn't matter how much of the world you see, at the end of the day you just want to come home. And then there's the whole business with Arthur – see, it's not him typin' this for me now for instance…

To be blunt, I've found this lovely boy called Vicente. He's done an English degree. He says hello. He's smilin'! Smilin' more now that he has to write this down! Anyway, the point is, Arthur thinks I'm demanding. (Actually accused me of bein' a nympho the other night, but I think that was more the tequila talkin' than him.) But anyway, that's private, and it's unfair that you have to hear it (and it's unfair for Vicente to have to type it, in all honesty).

Anyhow, people seem a lot happier here than us at home. Maybe a bit more content or somethin'. I don't know what it is. Now, don't you start worryin' ewer little arse off that I'm gonna do a Shirley Valentine on you. I'm definitely comin' back. See, that's the whole point – I am going, to come back. If you catch my drift?

But I tell ew what, this South America, there's somethin' about it. There is somethin' about it … Vicente's gonna take me for a cachapa now. It's a pancake apparently, but I'll be damned if that's all it is.

Love to you all, and a big hug to ewer Mam and little Gwen,

Peg, Arthur and Vicente xxxx

Not a word about Harry, I think to myself. Nothing at all. Bit weird, considering she made such a fuss about me takin' flowers to his grave.

Peg,
Good to hear back from you. I'm keepin' this short because I only want to know ONE thing. When are you plannin' on getting back? I'd really, REALLY appreciate it if you could just tell me. At least I'll know how long this is goin' to go on for then. Take care of ewer self and have a good time.

Love you, but let me know yeah?

Sam X

P.S. Are you takin' malaria tablets? I reckon maybe you ought to. Ask this boy to google it in Spanish. Don't want you dyin' on me.

It wasn't long before Gwen came out of the hall from practice that I saw Mr Pritchard. The last bell was about to ring, and he sort of just came out of nowhere.

'Hiya!' (Much too keen.) 'Christmas concert comin' on ok?'

He does this funny thing with his body then, indicating that he's about to collapse. I laugh, cos he's funny. Like Charlie Chaplin, only sexy.

'Like the fish head by the way.'

I throw him a sceptical look.

'No, serious. I thought it looked really convincing, actually. All that tin foil. Must have cost you a fortune …' and he's enjoyin' the fact that I'm laughin', I can tell. And I like that he's enjoyin' it. I can look really cute sometimes, even if I say so myself.

'Cymraeg,' I say then, because I know I have to practise. And secretly, I know I've got more of a chance with him if I say that, even if it is just a fantasy. He smiles and his whole face lights up and draws me in.

'Swimming lessons,' he says, as if he's clicked from a trance. 'Gwersi nofio,' he corrects himself. I smile. 'No go, I'm afraid.' He leans in towards me. 'Bloody county council. Nes i gynnig neud y gwersi 'yn hunan.'

'You teach swimmin' do you?'

'Well, no, ond gallen i. Ti'n gallu nofio?'

What a random question, I think to myself. Can I swim? We're getting desperate by here.

'Dim ond doggy paddle,' and I do this thing with my

hands. His turn to laugh this time. Only I wasn't tryin' to be funny. Doggy paddle is what I do.

I hate to admit it, but he seems ever so slightly distracted today. One eye on me and one eye on … hell, I don't know. It's all in my head anyway.

'Got all your shoppin' done?' Why did I ask that?

'Yeah. I'm dreading Christmas Day, mind,' he combs his flotsam and jetsam hair back with his fingers and looks through the window into the hall. 'My Mam's got this new obsession with knitting. God knows what she'll have made me. I think it's 'cos my brother and his wife are expecting their first.' He seems to click out of it then, as if he realises he's being too friendly with me.

'Listen, well i fi fynd 'nôl,' says he'd best get back.

As he walks away, all I can think about is the colour of his hair. Gingers and blonds. Suspended in the air. Like when you shake a sparkler in the dead of night.

Frustrated with the fact that he's gone, I turn my back. Some people you can never get enough of. You kind of thirst for every second you can get in their company. I try and snap out of it. Try and remind myself that we're from different worlds. Him living down Cardiff, going out for supper in posh restaraunts and getting the girls. Me, here with little Gwen. For a moment I feel hellish envious of him. It's an ugly feelin' that I don't want to get accustomed to. All that Welsh inside his head. All those things he can say that I can't. All that claim he has on things that are just out of my reach and always will be.

Soon enough, the last bell rings, and the kids come pouring out the hall, all dressed in their costumes. Miss Non comes out too, and Mrs Crouch. And then, there, behind them all, helpin' one of the tiny ones dressed as a prawn to get his navy blue coat on, is Mr Pritchard. He doesn't notice me again that afternoon. There's no point me even pretending that he does, because he doesn't. And why should he anyway? He's busy. Only there's still that tiny hope inside me, to be honest. That my light is still suspended in his head too. Because for some reason, I smell the future on him, even though that's completely impossible.

Eventually, my fish comes to find me and holds my hand.

'Take that fish head off now then love, or you might trip up.'

The fish shakes its head and talks in a strange muffled voice.

'I'm stayin' fishy.'

And being as I'm in a good mood, I respect her wishes.

♥

'What if he had asthmatack in the middle of bringing the presents?' she asks sleepily, her head resting on my shoulder.

'How d'you mean now?' I ask, comin' around the last bend on the stairs with a tiny ache in my back.

'Like if he falls and dies in the middle of it. Some children will get presents, and some will have to …'

'You don't have to worry about Siôn Corn. He can't really get ill. Doesn't work like that.'

'Callum said his Mam said Siôn Corn went to hospital last year, and that's why he was late to his house.'

As we head towards our front door, I spot him. Smokin'. Slumped over his own lap. He isn't lookin' out at Ponty, I think to myself. That just says so much.

'Dadi!' Gwen shouts, running towards him as he throws his fag over the fence.

'Gweni.'

'What you doin' here?' I try not to sound annoyed in front of Gwen.

'We had band practice up the Graig. Thought I'd stop by.'

Gwen grabs the fish head and holds it out for Richard to see.

'Look at my pysgodyn! Mr Pritchard said I'm the best one in the show.'

'Is it,' he says, before looking at me. 'Can I come in?'

'Yay!' Gwen screams as I reach for the keys. 'You can play the jigsaw game with me.'

As they push past me, I resent him. The way her love is so unconditional. The way he betrayed us like he did. The memory that never fades.

Hug me

Next morning, I'm in Argos, staring at the famous fat catalogue. As ever, it's jam-packed with things, things and more things. I look around and clock a load of people who are probably in the same situation as me. Buying Christmas presents for their children that they can't really afford.

I reach into my handbag for Gwen's letter to Siôn Corn. The note spells out exactly the type of karaoke machine she wants. I flick through the fatalogue then, until I get to the toys section. Heart attack central.

I notice that the man next to me seems to be searching through the toys too. He's got an interesting face, this bloke. All heavy in the jaw, as if he's from America. And he has diamond earrings in both ears too. Which I've never really liked on men if I was honest, but I must admit he sort of gets away with it.

Trying not to look too nosy, I turn my attention back to the fatalogue. The pink karaoke machine sticks out like a sore thumb. There's no way around it. This is the one she wants. Of course, there'd be no way in the world it would sound the same if it wasn't pink. As I spot the price, I sigh without realising. Ninety-seven bloody pounds it's going to set me back.

'Tell me about it love. I've got five kids,' drawls the bloke next to me. How does he know I don't have five kids too? Must be my youthful looks. Reluctantly, I slide my credit card out of my little purse and hover over the machine.

'Get it over and done with quick, love. That's what I'd do.' And so I type in the order number and submit my details. Standing there in all my layers, a cold sweat settles over my body. Too late now, I think to myself, you've done it.

As the information goes through the system, my phone rings. It's Arse. Soundin' a little downbeat.

'I'm in town too,' she says, after the usual pleasantries. 'Got time for a coffee?'

'In Argos, I am. Just waitin' to collect Gwen's present. After that, I'm free.'

'Number 562,' some lad shouts lazily from behind the counter. The way his voice sounds, I'm surprised he's managed to get himself out of bed this mornin', let alone come to work to shout out numbers. I head towards the counter where a pink tower cardboard box is waitin' for me. Because of you, I think to myself, we're gonna be skint through the *whole* of January. And the joke is, she probably will have stopped using you by the fifteenth. Nevertheless, I give the box a big hug in order to carry it out of Argos. I'm hugging my bloody debt, I think to myself. Only hug I've had in yonks.

I'm just headin' up the street when a young girl stops me and hands me a leaflet.

'Have you seen this woman?'

I take a quick look at the leaflet and clock Peg's face. Annoyed, I hand it back to the girl. March up the street to the sound of a plastic Santa Claus singing 'We wish you a merry Christmas'. I've got my moody face on now, I can just feel it sitting there. My forehead's stiff and my eyebrows are all furrowed. And then I hear his voice.

'Hei, ti,' I turn around and come face to face with flotsam and jetsam boy.

'Teachers don't need to be in school any more, do they?' I ask, clinging onto the box.

He smiles. Holds up two bags. 'Props for the Sioe Nadolig. Amser cinio.'

In desperation, I try my best to look as sexy as I can. I doubt even Naomi Campbell could pull this one off, to be fair. Single mother struggling. It's stamped across my forehead.

'T'ishe help?'

I shake my head, sweat profusely, smile.

'When are we gonna meet up, then?' he asks. Cool as a cucumber.

I stand there, stunned.

'We don't have to. Just thought we could go for a drink, that's all.'

'I don't come down Cardiff often.' Good job I'm holding a box, or else I'd have punched myself in the face for bein' so negative.

'Well that's alright then. 'Cos I live in Ponty.'

He puts his bags down for a moment, reaches into his pocket for a biro and scribbles on the cardboard box, cool as can be. Hair in his eyes.

'Here's my number. 'Case you change your mind.'

And then just like that, he picks up his bags, smiles and walks away. Only I can't move. Drunk with the light of him, I am, on this cold December day.

I'm sure I must look exactly like that guy who pretends to be a statue outside Superdrug. If there was a jumper in front of me, they'd be tossin' coins.

♥

I'm still thinking about Arwyn when I get to the café to meet Arse. Only she doesn't seem to be looking as jolly. There's no colour in her cheeks. Carly's sleeping in the buggy next to her.

'Ordered you a tea,' she says, as I head towards her, full of the joys of December. 'Waitress says she'll bring everything over.' As I put down the box I clock his scribbled number from the corner of my eye.

'Perry alright?'

'With Mam. She's taken him down Ogmore.'

'You alright? You look a bit peaky.'

'Run down,' she says, plonking a smile on her face.

'Not feelin' down are you? Winter can do that. Not enough light.'

'He hit me.'

And just as those words hit me, the waitress rocks up with an annoyingly cheery voice.

'Who's havin' the Coke?' Arse puts her hand up. 'And the tea?' Well that would be bloody obvious to anyone with half a brain cell.

'Enjoy your food, girls!' she says then as she waltzes away. Only, no one's got no food. And no one's gonna enjoy nothin'.

Arse doesn't look at me. I spoon sugar into my tea.

'Has it happened before?'

'Only when he was really hammered. Once. After this party up the council.'

The red of the Coke can in her hand makes me want to explode. The colour. The white fancy writing. 'It's the real thing'. The real thing. This is the real thing. By here. Now.

'You should have told me. First time round.'

'He was blind drunk. He couldn't even remember he'd done it the day after,' she lifts the can up to her mouth. Carly stirs in her chair, does a cute little whimper.

'He don't deserve you,' I say. Only I immediately regret sayin' it, because that gives her room to justify his actions and stick up for him.

'He's a brilliant dad. And let's face it, we wouldn't even have a mortgage if it wasn't for him.'

'What's a mortgage when it's at home?' She smiles a devastating smile at me. Sarcasm and guilt, mixed as one.

The smell of corned beef pasties fills my nostrils. Salt and vinegar crisps too. Waftin' over from someone else's plate. Hellish inappropriate smell. Hellish intrusive.

'I'm not leavin' him. Just in case you think. I'm gonna give him one more chance.'

'I wasn't even goin' to suggest it actually,' I say. Because I wasn't.

For the time bein', she's obviously a lost cause. Sorted it all out in her head.

I watch her as she fetches Carly from the buggy. Sneaks a peek at her phone. She obviously wants to leave. Even though I've only just arrived. Sayin' everything out loud has been too much for her, and she obviously hadn't planned on blurting it out.

'I better make a move soon. Got this parcel to pick up.'

I know full well that I won't see her for a while now. She'll shy away. Because that's what we all do when we're faced with facts that don't suit us.

'By the way, d'you remember Craig Darlow in school?'

'Camp?'

'Aye. But he's not gay. His Gran died yesterday. Apparently she fell head first into the road and a car knocked her over.'

'Bless her,' I say, as I envisage the scene.

Arse does a sympathetic face and heads off. I laugh to myself then, because I know what she's just done. She only went and gave me something else to chew on as she left. Arwyn's face floats into my mind again; butterflies fluttering by in my belly. I could never have brought it up with Arse just now. Not in the middle of all that mess. It's too light a thing to talk about. A stupid date. A stupid drink. Too nice a daydream to fit in with real life.

WILD THING

'What d'you mean, she's fine?' Mam's eyes narrow. I've brought her up to one of the Italian caffs in Treorchy in the hope that she won't make a scene.

'She's been in touch,' I stuff a chip in my mouth, sheepish. Try and avoid eye contact. 'I kind of know. Where she is. Where she was.'

'You *what*?' Mam takes a look around the café. Paranoid that someone has heard our conversation. She pushes her plate of faggots and chips to one side. 'You mean to tell me you've brought me all the way up to Treorchy to tell me she's fine?'

I swallow down the chip. My eyes wide open. No point closin' them anymore.

'What are the police gonna say?'

'The police are not gonna find out,' I punch out my words, looking directly at Mam. 'Unless you decide to grass her up, that is.'

Mam just sits there then. All limp like a gone-off lettuce leaf.

'That bleedin' woman's off her flippin … she could be done for robbery. You do know that.'

I nod at her. Yes, I've thought of this too, Mother.

'You should have told me. Before I had to go and see that damn dead woman's face.'

'It was too late, wasn't it? You'd already gone down the morgue by the time I came up the house.'

Mam stares hazily at her faggots for some time before popping her head up as if she's been under water.

'Where to is she, then? Cardiff?'

I shake my head slowly. Feel kind of excited about tellin' her.

'At the moment, she's in Venezuela.'

'Vene-where?'

'Zuela. It's in South Ame …'

'I don't care where it is,' Mam shakes her head again. 'Terry's gonna hit the roof.'

'You're not tellin' Terry.'

In a sulk, Mam grabs her fork and starts shoving chips into her mouth.

'Steady on, isit. You could choke on them.'

'Who cares,' she says, all potato and spit.

'I've asked her when she's thinkin' of comin' back. I should know soon. Then we can think of a plan.'

'Oh, fair play to her. Gonna have the courtesy to tell us what her plans are, is she? You do know we could all be in the shit, don't you? Wastin' police time.'

I nod at Mam and push her plate closer towards her. I'd rather see her shovel down chips again than listen to her tellin' me things I've already worried about in the dead of night.

'I've met this old man, too,' I say then. 'Peg's friend. She thought he was dead, turns out he's still alive.'

Mam rolls her eyes. What next?

'Is he a criminal?'

'What?! As if.'

'Well, you know how Peg is. All these different people she knows.'

'He's harmless, Mam. He's like a hamster. His name's Harry.' Mam stops then. Looks up at me.

I can tell by her face that this name means more than she's willin' to let on.

'They had an affair! I bloody well knew it.'

'Don't be so stupid.'

'How d'you know him, then?'

'He had a stall, didn't he. Down the market.'

'You just did a face like a horse, Mam. Spit it out, will you?'

'There's nothin' to say, love, except that they did nothing wrong.' And I know my annoying Mam well enough to know that I'm not going to get any further today. This is how she gets sometimes. When it comes to family business. All cloak and dagger. Nearly as if she's enjoying it.

I look down at my chips. Cold and insipid.

'I will be tellin' Terry about Peg, by the way,' she says then, 'he's family.' She wouldn't have been able to deliver a more annoying line if she'd tried.

'Please Mam. Fewer who know the better.'

'Don't worry. I won't be telling Gareth or Anj,' she says then, 'and Terry won't tell a soul.'

I stare her out then. Annoyed by the fact that it's her information to share now too. But at the end of the day, there's nothing I can do about it.

TELL ME

He opens the door in his slippers, and the first thing I notice is that his house smells like pine trees. That or antiseptic cleaning spray. I can't quite make it out. He has a study where he keeps all his paintings too, and that's where he takes me first. I notice as I go that he doesn't seem to have any of his own paintings on the other walls around the house. Suppose it's not the done thing, to stare at your own imagination all day. Bet he kind of fancies doing it sometimes though. I mean, come off it. Anyone who has enough of an ego to think he can draw must think they'd be good enough to look at.

He has a shaggy powder-green rug in the lounge, like wild grass by the fireplace. Only outside through the window, his lawn is cut as neat and low and tidy as a green mat. I don't understand people sometimes. Why they need to control nature like that.

'Let's go into the kitchen. Have a cup of tea.' So I follow.

I pour the tea, the gushing noise of the water from the spout filling the silence.

'Your house is lush.'

'It's a bit big for one person.'

We sip the tea and talk about various things. Richard. Work. How he's gettin' a new hearing aid. And then crunch time comes. That horrible heaving feeling, when you have to get something off your chest.

'So I told Mam. About Peg.'

And he nods in support.

'Only, turns out, it wasn't her that she was most interested in.' Harry purses his lips, unsure what I mean by this. In the silence, I look out at the lawn. Skim my eyes over the cool of the green grass. Try to remain composed. Then I turn back towards him.

'I know there's something you're not telling me. Can you please just tell me? I feel like a shit Miss Marple.' He smirks then. Amused by my ridiculous quip. Only he quickly resumes his serious face.

'It's all in the past now.'

'I really want to know, Harry.'

'I don't know whether it's my information to share, Sam. That's my problem.'

Harry sits there like a statue. Knows that he only has a few moments to decide what to do. Eventually, he looks straight at me.

'You won't tell your mother?'

'She knows!'

'But I don't think she wants *you* to know. Or at least, if she feels like me, she probably thinks it's up to Peg to tell you.'

'Peg's not here. Please Harry, just tell me.' He places his hands on the table, just like he did before. I watch as his Adam's apple goes up and down.

'Your Uncle Alf and Peg. They must have married

when they were both seventeen. Childhood sweethearts.'
And I nod. Because I've heard it all before.

'Alf was a singer in the cymanfas,' he goes on, 'very well known. Had this marvellous voice. Pure. I mean, I knew about Alf, even before I met Peg. Everyone knew him.'

'Nanna used to go on about him. How good his voice was.'

'Yes,' says Harry, with a sigh to match. 'Well, little by little over the years, I heard another story about him, I'm afraid. Turns out Alf was quite a different person when he wasn't parading down Treorchy high street on a Sunday. Your Nanna wouldn't have known that, perhaps, because Peg would have kept it quiet. And I mean, he was a big character. Could charm a red nose off a reindeer. Only Peg knew another Alf. And he was a nasty piece of work at times. Especially after a drink.'

I sit there trying to work out where this is going. He's just done a typically Welsh thing. Danced around the facts until you actually think you've just heard them.

'So did you fall in love? Is that what you're tryin' to tell me. Did you have an affair?'

'No,' Harry's voice is sombre. Annoyed even. 'We did become very close over the years, I can't deny that. Probably a little emotionally dependent too, if I'm honest, but it was nothing more than that. We were able to offload things, that's all. And we were alike. We both loved reading. And she'd take the time to look at my art. And she was very funny too. Cheeky. You know how she is. And, well, there wasn't always laughter in my marriage. But then, that's marriage. Hannah wanted me to go back to teaching. Didn't much care for my stall. But I was an awful teacher, you should have seen me! And you see, Peg understood. I'm not saying, perhaps it was easier for her, because she wasn't the one having to make do with my pay packet. But I just felt as if she understood.' He pauses for a moment, takes a sip of tea.

'Anyway, over the years, things became very difficult for Peg. Her and Alf were trying to start a family, and things weren't working out. And then in the space of two years, Peg lost two babies. It was a terrible time for her. Especially as your Nanna had two healthy children. One of them being your Dad, of course. I suspect that this was all getting to Alf too, looking back. Peg's expectations. Their quiet grief. His public persona. It can't have been easy. Not that that's any justification for how he behaved. But I suppose I'm just trying to understand how things got to where they did. Why he was so bitter and cruel.'

I look at the tea leaves. Notice how they've settled at the bottom of my tea cup. From what he's just said, I can tell that this isn't going to end well.

'Looking back, I think she hoped that having a child would change things. Make things easier between them. Of course, I knew it wouldn't change anything for the better. I'd made that mistake myself. But we always hope don't we, us humans, that something might come around the next corner and change things. And that was Peg's great hope too, I suppose. Sometimes I think the only reason hope was created was to make fools out of us.'

His words chime with everything I'm thinking at that moment. One tiny sentence that sums it all up. How foolish our hopes for tomorrow make us. How passive. How unwise.

'And then one day, Peg stopped visiting the stall,' he falters, remembers back. 'I didn't notice to begin with, but as time went by, it was obvious that something wasn't right. A week went by. A fortnight. And still no visit. Eventually, I came to the conclusion that I must have said something to offend her, or that perhaps she was expecting a baby again and didn't want to take any chances by traipsing down to Ponty just for the sake of buying a few stupid books and spending time with me. I missed her terribly. Began to understand how close we had become … And then one day, I decided to talk to Linda. She worked at the fruit and veg stall and she knew Peg from home. She told me that Peg had fallen down the stairs. It was a nasty fall, apparently, and she was in hospital with a broken hip. Only I knew straight away that there was more to it. I pushed Linda for the truth, but she wouldn't budge. Didn't think it was her news to tell. But I badgered her, eventually threatening to go up there to see Peg myself. And that's when she caved in.'

I watch Harry like a hawk. Notice every change of expression in his face. He doesn't even need to say what he says next as I already understand, by the look of disgust on his face.

'Alf had got wind of the fact that we were friends,' he announces, pointedly. 'Now I don't know how he found out, or what he knew previously, but that's what happened. And of course, he got it into his head that we were … oh, I don't know. Well, we weren't. But that's Ponty for you. Eyes and ears in the walls, even.'

My eyes are fixed on his now.

'I'm afraid Peg hadn't fallen down the stairs. Alf had come home from the pub one evening and had beaten her. Badly. Because of our "affair".'

Harry finds it hard to breathe for a moment. Makes a fist with one hand on the table. I sit there. Sad and useless.

'How long did he go to jail for?' Harry doesn't look at me. Just shakes his head.

'That's insane!'

'That's how things were, Sam. People just didn't tell the authorities. They covered things up.'

'The police must have known. People must have known.'

'Of course – everyone knew. I mean, she was in hospital for goodness knows how long. But the official line was that she'd fallen down the stairs, so that was that. Of course, everyone had heard the rumour. About our "affair". And about Alf's temper. But no one had any hard facts. So, as with any situation like this, what happens in the end is that all the facts and the rumours are gathered up together until they form one solid truth from start to finish. A story. A narrative that people can gossip about. Of course the affair had happened – it had just been covered up! After all, there's never smoke without fire, is there? And of course Alf had attacked Peg – it had just been covered up. By then it didn't even matter anyway. What was true and what was false. Because Peg had suffered the consequences.'

Harry looks spent now. Sat in his chair. All his energy escaped into the December air. Him like a sack of skin.

'Did you visit Peg? In hospital?' He shakes his head as if it's a heavy rock.

'It would only have added fuel to the fire. I asked Linda about her occasionally. Sent her a few books as presents. But we never saw each other again. Not once. I had that market stall for another ten years, but she never came by. The whole thing had been smashed to smithereens.'

'Where did Peg go? After that?'

Harry looks at me, confused by my question.

'She went home. To Alf.' I swallow my spit, look at him with a heavy heart. Why would she have done that?

'That's what happened in those days. Especially when you were financially dependent. The house was his. He had work.'

'She could have moved. Anywhere.'

'Where, Sam?'

'Nanna could have taken her in.'

'I don't know how much your Nanna knew. I think Peg tried her best to keep it from her.' Harry looks at me, aware that I'm saddened. 'I'm sorry.'

'Don't say sorry. There's nothing you could have done.'

'Maybe not. But that's why I was so glad. To hear that she was doing what she's doing. Travelling the world. Throwing caution to the wind. It's about time she got to do what she wants. She's waited long enough for it.'

'Spending Alf's compo. That's what she's doing now,' I say then, looking at Harry with a glint in my eye.

'Quite,' he says lifting up his tea cup. 'Bloody well quite. And about time too. The bastard swine. I hope he rots in his grave,' only as soon as he's said it, he looks up. 'Sorry. I don't mean to sound … Oh sod, it. He was a swine. A bloody bastard.'

And for a moment, I want to kiss him on the cheek. For having so much anger in him. And for loving Peg. Albeit as a friend.

'And when she's back, you'll be able to meet up,' I say then, with a smile in my voice.

'I know,' he says then, 'we will, won't we. Finally.'

And I watch him take his hands from the table. Placing them on his lap.

NEW LOVE

I'm staring in the mirror, about to apply my eyeliner as Gwen enters the bathroom.

'It's full up! Look!' She holds her little rucksack up for me to see. She's ever so excited that she's stayin' at Nanna and fat-man-Terry's.

'Well done,' I say, 'now pop ewer toothbrush in the front pocket for me, there's a good girl.'

She does as she's told as I stare at myself in the mirror. Look at my perfectly plucked eyebrows.

'Where you goin'? To a party?' She busies herself with her rucksack. For a moment, it's as if she's my mother.

'Aye. Mami's meetin' some friends.'

One friend, I think to myself. One special friend.

'I thought you was. You got the perfume on,' and she exits with her bag.

I run the eyeliner along the bottom of my left eye before grabbing a lipstick. I can't remember the last time I felt this excited. Shaved my legs. Used fake tan. I mean, I do remember, getting excited before meeting Richard. Right at the beginnin'. Actually, not right at the beginning, but about two months in. Only he went and wiped away all the make-up and washed away all the perfume when he decided to see that girl. Reckon I would have accepted it if it was a one-night stand. But six months is a long time to keep things behind your eyes.

I'm dragged back to the present by my bright and shiny pink lips and my long black eyelashes. Just then, Gwen marches back in on a mission.

'I think this will look pretty on you, Mam,' and she holds up one of my shiny necklaces from New Look.

I smile at her, and take it. Because she's absolutely right.

'We better get a move on,' she says then, tapping her wrist even though she isn't wearing a watch, ''cos Bampy gonna be waitin' for me, see. And I don't want to be late.'

The thought of her callin' Terry Bampy annoys me so much. Only I don't show it.

'Right you are. Come on then.'

♥

He's drinking Guinness. I'm drinkin' a vodka and coke. We're both smiling.

I've been laughin' too. Sometimes just because I know I *ought* to and sometimes because I've actually concentrated on the joke. It's not that I'm bein' rude or nothin', but I kind of enjoy zoning out every now and then to just look at him. Study his features. His flotsam and jetsam features. His light eyebrows that are hardly even there. I've decided I like his earlobes too. There's something special about those earlobes.

I tell him a few funny stories about Gwen then. Seems to me the only funny stories I've got these days are about little Gwen.

'Don't get me wrong. I do love her.'

'Glad to hear that.' First bit of English he's used all night. I laugh again.

Laughing is a funny thing. I remember once, I was listening to this funny guy on Real Radio in the bath when I sort of started dozing off in the warm, wet water. Even though I couldn't hear the words no more I still ended up laughing every so often because under the water the sound of it was still funny. It was more about the tone of his voice than what he *actually* said. I swear some people have perfected that art. Kind of like really caveman, isn't it. Singing your voice in such a way that other humans just have to sort of laugh. Like back when you were a baby, I suppose.

'Your Welsh is really good, Sam,' he says then. And there's the killer blow. He's said my name again. I swear some people can mesmerise you with ewer own bloody name. Stun you half alive with ewer own friggin' *name*.

'It's rusty, I know it is. Only I don't get no practice. They force you to speak it all through school and then you just stop.'

He smiles, and something strikes me. I actually think that a different me comes out when I say things in Welsh. It's like another memory opens up in my head. As if another part of my personality comes alive. And I wonder whether if I could speak loads of languages, whether I'd have tons of different memories. Tons of different personalities. I can't help but think that if he stuck around, my Welsh would be amazing. Little Gwen's too. I'd speak Welsh to her all the time then, because he'd be able to help me when I got stuff wrong. Only I don't even dare show that I'm thinkin' it. It would be too much like a dream come true if that would happen. We'd be like on *Pobol y Cwm*.

A couple of drinks later and we're doing the 'man and woman dance' thing. He's lookin' into my eyes more, I'm touchin' him, tellin' him he's funny, pokin' him in his chest, pretending to be offended. Laughing too much, making him feel like he's the funniest guy alive. All my eyes are on him now. I mean, I know I've only got two eyes, but I've got *more* eyes than that in reality. We all have. Those extra eyes that notice what's around the corner, those extra eyes that know what's goin' on behind you and who's due to text you. All those eyes have gone now. Suddenly, I've only got eyes for him.

'You've got pretty eyes,' he comes up close.

'Say it in Cymraeg,' I mutter, winding him up.

'Llyged pert 'da ti,' and he leans in towards me.

He's really close up now. Out of focus. Only he pulls back a little then, and I notice his eyes dance around playfully, before looking deep into mine. For a moment it's as if he can read my mind. I can hear his breath too. His Guinness breath and his blond hair. Filling up my senses.

And that's when, having lost all patience, I kiss him.

A soft touching of lips.

Like tissue paper.

Soft, like when you run sand through your fingers on a beach. Soft, like when your leg finds a comfy place to rub against under the sheets. I could stay there for a long while. I think we both could. But then we both hear this voice.

'Be sy'n digwydd fama, 'ta?' Arwyn pulls back. Looks up. A mate of his is standing there. Looks like a real rugby boy. I think he comes from north Wales, by his accent.

And suddenly, it's as if Arwyn has gone into his shell. A shell I didn't know he owned. He manages to introduce me and I smile. Turns out this guy's a teacher too. This ruddy-cheeked monster. I don't know what it is I don't like about him, but I feel like he's looking down on me. Straight away.

'You try and live with this one,' he exclaims.

'Is it?' I ask innocently.

'Can't keep up with him ...' and my heart sinks, because I'm bright enough to know what was hidden in that sentence.

Of course I am. Of course I'm one in a long list. Look at him. It would be criminal if I wasn't. And this bloke is obviously jealous. And a bit of a bastard too, for spelling it out.

We sit there then, chatting awkwardly. Gruff, as it turns out his name is, wants to know everything. What I do for a living. Where I live. What the fuck does it matter, I think to myself, only I don't show a thing.

As I finish answering, he smiles. 'Not comfortable speaking Welsh, no?' and I just want to punch him in the balls.

I listen to them chatter then. Something about getting a few items of food from M&S because they hadn't had a chance to go to Sainsbury's. Watchin' them, I feel as if we're worlds apart. I've never bought nothin' to eat from Sainsbury's, let alone Marks and Spencer.

I think about their Mams then. Try and guess what they're like. I've got this theory that Mams are at the root of every damn thing. At least that's how I see it. And men, especially men, perform to them, all their life. Dance on this stage for them. Try and live up to their expectations. Arwyn and Gruff's Mams must be Marks and Spencer Mams, I decide after a few seconds. They must be pretty posh and mega Welshy. I mean, don't get me wrong, I wouldn't buy my underwear anywhere else. But baked beans from Marks and Spencer? You got to be fuckin' kiddin' me.

♥

Marks and Spencer or not, I'm back at the flat. At his flat. And Gruff's in bed. He apologised about Gruff. Said he could be a right twat sometimes. Those were his exact words. I didn't really disagree. Just pulled an ambiguous grimace, hopin' he'd understand. Don't really want to come across as a bitch this early on.

I've come to the hasty conclusion that he's two people, this boy. Likes to mess with the middle classes, but feels more comfortable with the likes of me. Drunk as a skunk, I sit on his leather sofa tryin' to look sophisticated. Trying to entice him over to kiss me, which he eventually does.

After a while we take a breather, and he goes to get some drinks. I clock that this place could do with a good clean. A good dusting. Then I stare up at the huge widescreen that isn't on. Ugly as hell they are, these tellies that just cover up half of the wall. And when he returns with drinks, I tell him that. He laughs, kisses me. Lips like soft bread rolls. My belly's gone weak with the fun of it. He says sorry they haven't got wine glasses. Only mugs.

As I sip, I spot the packet of Love Hearts in my handbag. Without thinking, I take them out and offer him one, playfully.

'Not one for sweets,' he says, and I help myself. A yellow loveheart with pink writing and a pink heart-shaped rim. I read the message in silence and pop it in my mouth.

'Be' odd e'n dweud?' he asks inquisitively.

'I don't remember,' I say, chewing on the chalky sweet.

He chuckles. Truth be told, I'd rather die than tell him what the message really said. In fact, as I swallow it down I realise what a stupid bloody idea it was, bringing them out in the first place.

Feeling a bit awkward, I head over towards the window and look out at Ponty. I'm getting to see town from another angle tonight. My feet are killing me in these heels, so I rest my hands on the window ledge just next to a model of a rugby player kicking a ball.

I hear him getting up from the sofa, only I don't show. I just keep looking out at Ponty. Pretty, pretty Ponty. All darkness and light. As he kisses the back of my neck I try and push it to the back of my mind that I'm one in a long list. After all, he could stop with me, couldn't he? I mean, everyone's got to stop somewhere…

As I yearn for my body to be pressed down upon, he draws the curtains. Nos da, Pontypridd, I say to myself, as I turn around to kiss him. Nos da.

LOVER

It must be about five o'clock in the morning, but we're still awake. Wide awake like children in a midnight feast. Wide awake like Romeo and Juliet. I'm sure I remember reading something like that in school. How they're up at the crack of dawn one morning, holding each other and making the most of the early hours when who you are, where you're from and who you're related to doesn't matter at all.

'What you doing?' he asks, in a husky voice, his eyes shut for a moment.

'Nothin'.'

'You're starin'. I can feel it.'

He seems to want to swallow me up too, mind. Holding my hand. Touching my fingers as if he's never felt fingers before.

'You got a nice room.'

'It's pitch black, mun.'

'No it's not. And anyway, I got good eyes.'

'Have you now?'

'Eat loads of carrots.'

'That's why you look so tanned, is it?'

'Oy!' I say and I push my palm into his face, laughin'. 'You make me sound like a slapper or somethin'.'

'Joke, isn't it! If you were orange, I wouldn't tell you, would I?'

'I don't know. Maybe you would. Maybe you're a bastard.'

He sighs for a moment. Sleep filling his mind again.

'Maybe I am,' only I can hear his smile in his voice.

'I knew you might be the moment I seen you. 'Cos of ewer hair.'

'Is it now,' he says with a scoff, before rolling onto his side to face me.

In the half light, I can just about make out the huge poster he's put up. A surfer riding on a gigantic tidal wave. Skimming across this wall of water. That's how I feel with him. As if I'm surfing a wave that I know could come crashing down any minute. Only I battle against that feeling. Really, really hard. Because there's no reason things can't finally work out for me. No reason at all.

Just then, Arwyn plants a kiss on my forehead. A kiss that seems to mean more than just your average kiss. At least that's how I take it. A kiss that seems to indicate that maybe I could mean more to him than the other girls that have slept in his bed.

'Sleep now, is it?' he asks, turning over to the other side.

I lean towards him, kiss him gently on the nape of his neck. 'Siarad Cymraeg to me …'

'You're a funny one, Sam Jones,' he says then, all smiles and sleep. 'Cysga.'

And the sound of him sayin' my name hypnotizes me again. Lulls me into a deep, dreamless sleep. Where there is no language.

Break Me

Sam darlin',

Thanks for the last message. It was a bit short. I take it that means everythin's fine? God, I do hope everythin's OKAY on ewer side, and that there haven't been some sudden nuclear disasters or somethin'. I mean, it doesn't say anythin' on BBC News online, but then they're not always up to speed, are they?

Now, I don't want you to get annoyed with me, right, but I left Arthur in Venezuela. He was havin' a fab time down some of the bars and he tells me he thinks he's met his soulmate. This girl. Anna her name is. Travellin' from Australia. Now, I'm NOT on my own, before you start worryin'. Vicente has been kind enough to come with me down Argentina way. Well, I tell you Sam, I've been dancin' with him – I feel like I'm seventeen again! The tango in Buenos Airies, can you bloody well believe? With a hot-blooded male like Vicente (he's blushin' by here). It's so up close and steamy Sam, you would not BELIEVE! And all the oldies are up to it over by 'ere see. The tango, I mean. They're all queuin' up to get on the dance floor. And you dance with ewer partner like you bloody well mean business.

Last night we danced until eleven (three hours solid), his body against mine. The accordion, the piano, the bass, the cello, the violin. Rum-pum-pum-pum, rum-pum-pum-pum, rumpum rumpum, rumpum, rum-pum-rumpum. There's this lovely little marchin' rhythm and then a little flurry in the middle, see. Oh, you'd love it Sam cariad, you really would. And last night, I'll tell you because I love you, I was made love to, like ... well, you'll just have to imagine. The latin way, my love. The latin way. Arms and legs flyin' about. Sweat, blood and tears (no blood and no tears but I just wanted to put it in 'cause the rhythm sounds good). I tell you, the closest thing you might be able to describe it like is how Brad Pitt makes love to Thelma in Thelma and Louise. I mean, Arthur wasn't bad, but he was lackin' in confidence, you know ...

Incidentally, Vicente here is thinkin' about comin' back to the Rhondda with me. Could do me the world of good to have him about. Says he's always wanted to come to England, so obviously I've been educatin' him a bit about Wales and all that. Told him he'd be better off with us, bein' as we got free prescriptions.

Now, to answer your question about when I'll be back, I don't think I'll be back by Christmas to be honest. Thing is love, I'm having such a scream. You wouldn't blame me, would you? Would you, love? If I came back early in the new year?

144

And before you start worryin', I know I'm gonna
be in the shit, but I'm sure I'll be able to persuade
the authorities that I did nothin' wrong, and that
I had absolutely nothin' to do with the robbery
(delete this e-mail!!)

   Anyway, please let me know that everythin's
OKAY with you. I mean, Vicente here's been tellin'
me to stop biting my nails, but it's because I'm
worried about you, see.
Bye my darlin', to the beat of the tango,
Peg y Vicente xxxx

♥

Travellin' on the bus to work, I notice how dark a day it
is. Some days in December are like this. It's as if the day
just doesn't wake up. It's as if everything's sort of slowin'
down for Christmas Day.

I shuffle into Glanvillas, hopin' no one will notice that
I'm five minutes late. Bosh is sitting in his usual spot,
only he doesn't seem to have been handed his toastie yet.
Miracle of miracles, there's three old women sittin' on
the front table too. I'm chuffed. I mean this might make
all the difference for our shifts. New faces like this. New
people. New pound coins from new hands.

Pauline and Carol are busy getting little white teapots
ready.

'Are they havin' Italian?' I ask Carol.

'Nope. Same old, same old, only I'm putting them

145

down in the book as tapas,' she says in a glum tone. I clock that Pavarotti is still moaning in the background.

'One man did ask for the squid, mind,' Pauline reminds Carol tentatively.

'Aye, but it was by accident, Pauline. He meant to say quid, asking how much somethin' cost he was … oh, anyway, what the hell does it matter?' Carol turns towards me. 'I take it you've had the call.'

My eyes narrow. From who now?

'He's shuttin' up shop.'

I stand there. Stunned.

'He's lost the heart,' says Carol then. 'And once you've lost the heart …'

As I stand there, numb, I watch Carol picking up the tray full of little white teapots. I don't understand humans sometimes. It just seems so senseless that she'd still be busyin' herself with work. Still getting to it, struggling away.

Just then, Mr Twat Face comes in through the door.

'Sam,' he says, as soon as he sees my face. 'Can you come out the back?'

Only I'm not in the mood to obey orders today.

'By here'll be fine,' I say, starin' straight at him. 'So, you're closin' then.'

'You've heard. I did try phonin' you.'

'So, what? You're sellin' the buildin', are you?'

'Early days yet. But, I'm sorry is the first thing.'

'Sure, the hell you are.'

He sighs then. Not in the mood for this tension.

'It's tough for us all,' he says into the dead air.

'Not really quite as tough for you, though, is it? I mean, you've got your other businesses.'

He just stands there, looking at me.

'Took your eye off the ball here, once you got them hairdressers. Saw it happenin'. And haven't you got a haulage business too? That's what my brother told me.'

'Don't make it sound like I don't give a shit, Sam. 'Cos I do. This place have been keepin' me up at night.' The other girls look at us. Worried it's goin' to turn into a huge motherfuckin' argument.

'Should have just listened to your staff though, shouldn't you? I mean, did you ever really think this Italian business out in ewer head? No, you didn't.'

'Listen, Sam. I've said it before. You could be a manager. Go back to college, go to uni, even. My youngest is goin' in September, and you're way sharper than her.'

'And when d'you suppose a single Mam on benefits is gonna get time to study? When she's on the toilet, is it?'

And that's when it hits me. Right between the eyes. I'm going to come up against people like him all my life. People who've got things, can get things. People who've got just about enough money to spend themselves out of problems.

'That's all we ever wanted were the jobs you gave us in the first place, Glanville.' And I leave him there, standing on his own like a pillock.

I sit staring at a bowl of sugar for a while after he's gone. Try to make sense of it. The other girls don't disturb me for a bit. They know how I get sometimes.

Only after a while Pauline comes over to sit by me.

'Cheer up, mun.'

'Nothin' to be cheery about,' I say pushin' the sugar bowl away with my knuckles.

'Least we've got our health.' She's so wet she could run out of a tap, I swear. I hate the way she just accepts things.

I study her hands for a moment. Look at her wedding ring. Her carefully filed nails. She's the type of woman who thinks that most people are better than her. I mean, she probably actually thinks that Glanville knows best. Suddenly, I realise how depressed she makes me feel. More so than Glanville does, even. Her little cupid mouth. Her lips that always seem so red, even though she doesn't wear lipstick.

In the background, I hear Carol banging things about behind the counter. Just then, an idea crosses my mind. There's hope in Carol, I think to myself. I head towards her, my lungs filling up with the future again.

'Why don't we do what those baker boys did, Carol? Do it ourselves, like.'

'That was telly love,' Carol says, wiping the tops.

'No. John Lewis do it too. We could buy the place off Glanville. Or rent it off him.'

'Don't be daft now.'

'It's not daft. We could get people to buy shares.

Turn the place into what we want it to be. Sell books. Whatever.'

'People don't buy books these days love. They've all got Kindles.'

I breathe in with all my might. Try my hardest to make her see sense.

'Seriously, Carol. We could do this.'

Carol pauses for a moment. She can feel the desperation in my voice. She can tell that I'm on the brink.

Only I can see the words spilling out of her before she says them. Her whole body spelling it out for me. Heavy. Like an obstacle you could never budge even if you had the strength of a hundred horses.

'It's all over, bach.'

We glance at each other for a moment. A strange sadness washing over me. Not sad like you feel when someone dies. Not sad like when someone you love doesn't love you back. But this little ache, like a bad tummy. Dulling you. Making you wonder what it's all actually about.

I sit down again. Try to gather my thoughts. Only I feel shattered. For a moment, I cling to the thought of Arwyn. The one positive thing in my life right now. This new wind that's come gliding in from the sea. If it wasn't for that little bit of hope, I don't know where I'd be today, I really don't.

Picture Me

Being unemployed is great for the first week. It feels like a holiday. It's after that that it really begins to kick in. And when I say kicks in, I really mean it. It's as if, one night, you're lying in bed under a lovely duvet, and the next thing you're being hurled out onto a choppy sea of fear and panic. How are you going to pay the bills? What would be the worst case scenario? Where can we scrimp and save?

Of course, it's only a matter of time before all this leaves its mark on your body. The way you breathe. The way your eczema comes back to haunt your arms. The way you look at others. Envy them. Feel hard done by. In the end, being without money becomes a prison. An obsession. The root of all your ills.

It was the Tuesday after my Monday night panic attack that I saw Harry again. He'd called me a few days before and asked whether I'd like to meet for a Christmas sherry. I'd issued an automatic yes because that's what you do when someone old is being kind. But truth be told, as I travelled down on the train that morning I began to begrudge the fact that I was going. Probably because I couldn't really afford the fare.

When he hands me it, I cringe. Sherry on my breath.

'I can't take it.'

'Of course you can.'

I didn't tell him I was out of work for him to hand me a present. I look at the painting again. It's the one we saw at the gallery. With the crimson sunlight slicing through the trees.

'It's kind of you, but seriously …'

'It's been a pleasure to get to know you, Sam. Consider it a Christmas present.' I sit there. Thankful but hellish envious. This man who has money and freedom. This man who can just hand over a three hundred pound painting.

'I've been thinking about January. When Peg's back,' he says then, purposefully. 'I want us all to go out for a meal.'

I nod, and as he rambles on, revealing all his thoughts, I realise that he's the kind of person who doesn't really feel the need to consult. But more than that, I begin to realise how lonely he is. Peg has filled a convenient little gap in Harry's life. This whole story is going to take him through the winter. These plans. This newness. This purpose. And that's when I stop feeling envious of him. Because no-one ever has it all. Some of us are skint and some of us are lonely. All scrambling about like those puppies, blind and desperate for the light.

'I'll be back from Rhys's house by the second so we can go from there,' he announces.

'Where does Rhys live then?'

'Brighton.'

I nod. His one son. Far away in Brighton. Please don't make me begin to dislike Harry, I say to God. Only I know how my mind's working at the moment. It's feeling battered and bruised and hard done by, so it's finding the worst in people rather than the best. It's seeing through people's good deeds to the needs that they have. The selfish needs of finding a place to fit in. That need to be needed. And in this case, Harry's need to lay down the law to lonely.

I head up the path holding the painting. Wave back at him.

'Merry Christmas!' he shouts.

'Nadolig Llawen!' I say with a smile, before heading to the bus stop.

Sam,

Take it you got my message about comin' home in the New Year??! Me and Vicente are havin' a good time just chillin' out at the mo. Last night we just went to sit in a little café and talked all night about the dreams we had left to live. And one of mine is I want to take up graffiti. Like go on a course. I really do like the things that that Banksy boy does. Mind, he could be a girl. You never know. It could be me...

I've been teachin' Vicente some Welsh words too. Things like cariad and helô and hwyl fawr. We've had a hell of a laugh, and d'you know something? No one around here questions us. It's hellish refreshin', I tell you.

I can't tell you how nice it is to feel the heat of the sun all warm on my face in the mornings. Makes me feel like I'm a little plant, growing and growing. I'm just angry with myself that I haven't done this until now.

Now listen, I hope you don't mind me offloading all this on you but I've had a fantastic idea. I get so much time to think here, I've decided I should tell you some things I've discovered while I'm out here. And the weird thing is, right, they're mostly about home. How I should have lived my life. How I should have appreciated some things I had. So, here's what you're having for today: Enjoy the alive people. Enjoy them alive. (I enjoyed Alf much more once he was gone. But that's another story really.) By the way, Vicente doesn't think he'll be coming back with me to Wales. And there was you thinking he was some sort of granny-grabber! Out to get a visa. No. Vicente thinks we should keep our relationship a travelling relationship – I could always come back out see, couldn't I. His father was a teacher you know, but Vicente left home young because his next door neighbour threatened to kill him for sleeping with his girlfriend. He is adamant that they were very unhappy and that the bloke was seeing other people. But see, like I told him, the trouble with sleeping with your neighbour's wife is that they're always going to live next door. Least he could've done was choose

someone from the next town over. Daft dick. But
hey, we're all human, aren't we.
Anyway, I have posted a card, I hope it'll get to
you before Christmas Day!
Peg y Vicente
Xxxx

♥

I read this poem in school once. I don't even remember who wrote it now, but it made me sick with feelin'. Some poems did that to me in school. And I don't know whether it was really the words or the weight I put on them. All those hormones, churning around in me, that's what it was probably. But these words, right, in this particular poem I read in year nine, they were dripping so heavy with meaning, I nearly drowned. It was like I had my face in a puddle of words.

I don't understand why they don't tell you that in school. Why they don't tell you to hold on tight to your emotions before you read a poem. If you ask me, they should put a warning sign or a sticker on the front cover. 'These poems by here have very strong imagery, and you could end up feeling some heavy shit after reading them.' But no. They don't do it. Because that would be much too imaginative.

I'm talking about poetry because of a Christmas card that arrived this morning and changed things a bit … It must have landed on my floor while I was up Mam's. And it must have flown through the letterbox at quite a speed 'cos it landed a fair way in on the carpet.

> Despite the Christmas cheer,
> remember every year
> that what we should cherish most of all
> might not, for long, be here.

Now granted, that's a really shit poem. But sometimes it takes a shit poem to remind you of the good ones.

The Christmas card inside was pretty average too. A picture of a puppy dog lying in front of a fireplace. Tinsel on the mantelpiece, little stockings hangin' on the corners. And through the windows, you could see that it was snowing outside. Just like no fuckin' Christmas you've ever experienced in your life.

It's only when I see the handwriting that I realise who it's from.

> *Sorry about the crap poem. Too much time on my hands. Here it is, my darlin', my merry Christmas to you. Will you have a lager shandy and think of me? And will you try and listen to the carols from church on Christmas Eve? It's on the radio it is. Hellish Christmassy. Live and all.*
>
> *Will be going to a few nice places over the Christmas period. Apparently, Brazil is a good idea. Vicente fancies takin' me fishin', says he thinks it will be good for my soul. Now, you might think that there's me bein' funny with words, but*

actually, he did say that ('course, Vicente didn't
get the joke at all. He struggles with humour in
English. Second language and all.)
Anyway love, I love you all.
Cariad,
Peg (and Vicente says Nadolig Llawen too – I
taught him well, see!)

I hold the card tight. This cardboard's been further than
I've ever been, I think to myself. I smell it then, because
no one's lookin'. See if I can smell Peg. See if I can smell
South America. Then, I take it over to the little white
cabinet next to the telly and I pop it behind a photo of
Gwen dressed as a pirate. If anyone saw this card, I'd be
dead meat.

As I stand there looking at the photo of Gwen,
remembering all those things that happened the summer
she wore that costume, I start looking at her face in a new
light. If I'd gotten pregnant the night before I conceived
Gwen, would it still have been Gwen that came out? I
mean, it's a funny thing, but I've never thought of it like
that before, like. I mean, seriously now, is it all in the luck
of the draw who you end up being and end up becoming?
Or are you always the person who's goin' to pop out?
Of course, this makes me think about life and God and
weird things then. Things like, it's obviously meant to
be you, it can't all be left to chance. I mean, a minute
later? An hour later? That urge to get ewer legs around
someone is interrupted by *Casualty* or the *X Factor* final,

and you create a new person altogether? Could Simon Cowell really be responsible for the type of baby I have, for the type of story I add to my family tree?

I'm so fucked up with the idea of it all bein' one big chance situation that I just push the thought to the back of my head. Some things are too big to think about sometimes.

As I stop daydreaming, I realise I'm still holding onto Peg's envelope. And that's when it registers. The stamp. It's got the Queen's face on it. The messy, inky stamp doesn't say Brazil on it either. It says Rhondda Cynon Taf. And as exotic as that may sound to someone in Brazil, that's where I live. In Cymru / Wales.

I grab my mobile and text her. *Are you back?!*

And swear to God, as soon as I've sent it, I get one back. My heart skips a beat.

Rhondda Heritage Park Hotel. Peg x

Dream on

I can't stand the fact that I've had to ask him for help but fat-man-Terry's up here in a flash. He says there's some boxing highlights on from the weekend anyway, so he's happy to watch Sky in peace without Mam. He's a bit disappointed to hear that Gwen's sleeping, but I told him she was in a foul mood and that he wouldn't have wanted to see her like that anyway. If she wakes up, he should give her hot Ribena and send her straight back to bed.

As I grab my handbag, Terry tells me to enjoy my date. I smile, before disappearing into the dead of night. Like a detective on drugs.

♥

Before I know it, I'm sitting next to a teenage boy with bad BO on the bus to the Heritage Park. It's so freezing cold, I have to constantly wiggle my toes in my shoes to keep them warm. Where've you been that's warm enough to sweat? I think to myself, as BO boy continues to waft his unique aroma around the bus. This bus that couldn't go any slower if it tried. Just then, another message appears on my phone.

Need to speek bout Gwen's Xmas present. RX

The fact that he can't spell makes me sick. The fact that I want it to be a message from Arwyn makes me sicker.

Why hasn't he been in touch? I texted him four days ago. Just in time, I spot the Rhondda Heritage Park on my left and press the red stop button on the handrail in front of me. Then I head down the bus, thankin' God that she's home safe.

♥

As I get to the reception, the woman behind the counter smiles at me.

'Samantha Jones, is it love?' I nod, a bit confused, and she starts typing something on the computer. There's a huge Christmas tree behind her, but this woman by here's way more interesting than the decorations. It's like she's a receptionist by day and a bizarre woman who rules the world by night. And it's night-time now, so that would make sense. Her ginger hair sits like a flame on her head. Wrapped up in the most fantastic manner. Pinned tight. Hairsprayed. I move onto her face then, and I can't stop looking at her tiny freckles. Ginger freckles and white skin. Only soon enough, the big question starts zinging in my head again. Where the *hell* is Peg? And what do you know that I don't, you woman with hair that holds the secrets? Un-pin ewer hair, I say in my head, let those secrets out from behind those lacquered-cardboard pieces of ginger hair slices. C'mon, mun. Out!

Just then she leans in and whispers.

'She doesn't want people to know she's here,' her words pebble-dash desperately against my ears. I mean, it doesn't matter how quietly she says this. I'm all ears.

Seriously ALL ears (which obviously reminds me of being 'all eyes' with Arwyn the other night, which reminds me again that he still hasn't been in touch).

'How long 'as she been back?'

Ginger woman looks confused. 'Um. I don't know. She's been here a while now.' She pushes a hairpin so deep into her mop it's as if she's piercing her own skull. After sorting her hair, she presses some buttons, the white of the computer screen reflected in her eyes.

Just then, she looks up.

'Room 32. Four knocks.'

I head for the lift with the words 'four knocks' reverberating in my head, and for a second I feel like I'm actually in a James Bond film. In fact I feel so weird, I honestly wouldn't be surprised if Daniel Craig were the one answering the door to me.

♥

Knock. Knock. Knock. Knock. Knuckles on door. Thin skin on bone. I'm so self-aware, it's as if I'm two people. One of me is looking down at me doin' what I'm doin' and the other one is just feelin' like a tit.

'Is that *you*, love?'

The sound of her voice hits me. I can't believe it's actually her.

'Peg, mun. Let me in.'

And with that, the door opens and I step into the room. Into her world.

I stand there for a moment. Staring at her. She hasn't

changed one bit. She's in a little smock dress and slippers. And she's slapped on a full face of make-up too. Only despite of all the effort she's gone to, I can't help but notice that she's looking a bit frazzled.

'Peg, mun,' I say again, before giving her an awkward hug. As soon as we're in the embrace we're out of it. There's something so cringe about the touching of skin sometimes.

I notice that the room is quite poky. Clock her little leather suitcase next to the bedside cabinet.

'When did you get back? I thought you said you weren't comin' back till the new year.'

She looks at me for a moment, then looks at the floor. Her eyes showing nothing but eyeshadow. Lids, lids, lids. Only I want to see her pupils.

'Must have been tough. Leavin' Vicente behind.'

Peg doesn't move a muscle. I fear for a moment that she might start cryin'.

She takes a sharp breath before looking straight at me. Her light blue eyes dazzling.

'I haven't been *completely* straight with you.' In that silence before she carries on, I swear I imagine about four hundred different outcomes. Has she murdered Arthur? Is Vicente in the bathroom?

'I never went travelling.'

Her words buzz around my head for a moment. Like flies.

'What d'you mean, you never went travelling? You've been e-mailin'.'

'Yeah. From by 'ere.'

'What? You haven't even been to Barcelona?'

She shakes her head again.

'But what about Vicente? And fuckin' Arthur?!'

'He used me. To get the code for the safe.'

There's a fat silence then. Like a heavy continental quilt on a hot, clammy night. As the truth begins to ring in my ears, I sit down on the bed.

'I thought you were there, like. D'you know what I mean?'

'I did go to Bristol. That's where Arthur finished with me.'

Only I'm still angry with her. Because my truth is different.

'All those *things*, though. All those facts about Venezuela.'

'Google. Have you seen Google Earth, by the way? It's bloody phenomenal.'

'Everyone's been worried sick about you, mun!' I take a moment to breathe, but the thoughts just keep comin'. 'I've seriously imagined you there,' I say, disappointed.

'Can't you just pretend that I have been?'

'No. I fuckin' well can't.'

She looks at me then. Half upset, half amused.

'The girl down reception's been hellish nice,' she says in a sweet voice. 'Mind, I've had to pay her a fair bit. She thinks I'm in hiding.'

'You *are* in hiding.'

'Aye, but they think I'm in hiding from the KGB for …'

'Oh, shut up, Peg. I've had enough of your shit for one day.' And that's when she starts to laugh the walls down. Laughs so hard that her cheap mascara streams across her cheeks like spiders' legs. I swear she's from another planet.

'There is one more thing,' she says then, wiping her mouth with the back of her hand.

'What now?'

'Are you still in touch with Harry?' Her eyes glisten, and I nod. 'Promise me you'll never tell him the truth.'

I sigh. To be honest, I don't feel like I owe her no promises after all the crap and lies she's just dealt out.

'Alright,' I say eventually, only she doesn't seem to think I'm taking her seriously enough.

'Promise, Sam,' she says again. Firm.

'I won't tell him, alright? Now get your things, you crazy loon. We're goin' home to face the music.'

Gee Whizz

Peg and I sit on the sofa, drinkin' hot milk. Like two naughty schoolgirls. Her little leather suitcase next to my feet.

'First thing tomorrow, I'm takin' you down the police station so you can tell 'em what really happened. That Arthur ought to be hung, drawn and quartered.' Mam frowns.

Peg sips her milk, deliberately trying to give herself a moustache.

'All I can say is that I'm sorry,' she says, frothy tash in full view. 'I should have just come home straight away. Only I was humiliated, see. By that brute.'

Mam gives Peg one of those looks. Don't milk it now.

'When'll you be takin' me back up the Home, Janet?' Peg asks then, tryin' to convey a deep respect for Mam. Her light blue eyes wait for the answer.

Silence then, before Mam sighs. 'You can stay here over Christmas. But you're goin' back after. D'you hear me?'

A huge smile spreads across Peg's face. 'We'll have to get some eggnog in!'

Only Mam's not in the mood for her antics, 'You got milk all over you, Peg. Wipe it off.'

'Sorry Janet,' says Peg, her eyes dazzling. Annoyed, Mam gets up and heads for the kitchen.

On our own, Peg smiles a mischievous, milky smile at me.

'You're *actually* mental,' I say, starin' back at her.

'We're gonna have one hell of a Christmas,' she says then, gigglin' to herself.

Ever yours

We're all in the same row. Squashed together on uncomfortable plastic seats. Mam, me, Terry, Peg, Richard, Gareth and Anj. Only there's someone else in here too. And all my invisible eyes are on him.

All the kids are lookin' mental, dressed up like characters from the sea. The prawns are obviously tired because they've been stood on the stage for ages now. I clock Magdalen Maguire, who was in school with me, on the left hand side of the stage. She works for the media now and she always films the cyngerdds for the school. Done well for herself, she has. Works out for some people. My eyes settle on some blue tinsel for a moment. I don't know what it is about blue tinsel, but it really makes me feel Christmassy. I think it's because it's so fake-lookin'. So out of this world.

From where I'm sittin', I can hear Arwyn talking to the kids. And I can hear the kids chattering to each other too. Every single one of them in Welsh. I used to be like them, I think to myself. I don't know where or when it changes. But one day, just like that you don't do it no more.

Fat-man-Terry is looking very dapper tonight. Excited to be at the concert. That-man-from-down-the-Legion, that's who he'll always be to me. But that's not who he is to Gwen. He means more to her than I could probably imagine.

Being as she's achieved local celebrity status now that she's back, Peg is dressed to the nines. Sporting a green frock and bright purple eyeshadow. She's gone to town with her eyebrows too. Pencilled them in shakily, leaving two black arches above her eyes. Reckons she looks a million dollars. And in a way, I suppose she does.

All the fish and the seaweed and the octopuses are streaming onto the stage now. One little girl's cryin' her eyes out and Daniel from Gwen's class is pickin' his nose so deep that you nearly can't see his little finger. Just then, Gwen appears. Fishy foil head in full view.

'There she is, there!' I whisper to Mam, leaning forward in my seat. I can tell that everyone in this damn place is doin' the same. Searching for their daughters. Looking out for their sons. Thinking they stand out something special. I watch Gwen take off her fish head and search the audience for us all. It doesn't take her long to spot us. Smiles like she's never smiled before.

'Daddy!' she shouts then. And he waves back.

It isn't as if anyone else in the hall has noticed her shouting, because there's half a dozen others doin' exactly the same thing. Only I notice. And I know it's hellish childish of me, but I can't help but think – Daddy? The one who's let us down. The one who turns up when it suits him. Is that really who you're most glad to see?

Miss Non starts playing the out-of-tune piano then, and the lights go down. And before you know it every boy, girl, prawn and piranha in this hall starts performing for their Mams. Just like they always do. Even if they have just ignored them.

♥

'A dyma fe!' one of the angel fish shouts at the top of his voice.

'Babi!' the prawns shout and the fish around the cradle start swaying back and forth.

'Jesus the jellyfish!' one of the prawns shouts. 'Iesu Grist!' And this thing that looks a lot like a bag of placenta comes out from under Mair Marinara (the mother of Jesus the Jellyfish, obviously).

'Three king prawns from the east will come soon,' shouts a boy from the English department. 'Tri king prawn o'r dwyrain,' a little girl screeches. Even before she's finished reciting the line, she turns to her Mam for praise. I watch her smiling to herself, fat with her family's admiration.

'And bugeiliaid, shepherd's pies,' another says and a few girls next to him correct him. 'Noooo Kyle! Not shepherd's pies. Shepherds!' and the audience erupts in a united belly laugh (glad to get a chance to get it out of our systems, to be truthful). I catch a glimpse of Gareth. He doesn't look all that amused. Probably wants to get back home to watch some telly. And I can't say I blame him, really. I mean, if your own child wasn't in this show, you'd probably think you were on LSD.

'It's nobblin' out here,' Peg's black eyebrows shiver in the cold.

'I told you you should have stayed inside, mun.' Only she isn't listening. We're stood waiting at the back of the hall for milady to come out with her friends. She made an extra special effort tonight, so I want to give her a big, fat hug. Of course, I'd be lyin' if I said I didn't know that Arwyn could appear at any moment too. And so I'm standing as upright as I can. Just in case.

But Gwen's the first one out, with her slicked-back, ponytailed hair.

'Who's a clever girl then?' Peg shouts.

'Brilliant! Da iawn ti!'

As soon as Gwen spots Peg, she starts behaving all shy and annoying. It must be something to do with the eyeshadow. And the eyebrows. And the hair …

'Did you see me?'

I pick her up even though she's too heavy. "*Course* we saw you! You were seren y sioe.'

And that's when he comes out. Turning his head as he hears me. He looks awful tired. As if he's been in the sea for too long.

He throws me an awkward smile. Knows he hasn't been in touch. But I'm not goin' to make him feel guilty. I mean, he's been hellish busy. And it's not too late.

Gwen wriggles herself out of my arms, announcing

that she wants to see her Dad. Arwyn's too close now not to have heard. As she darts off, Peg follows her. Only I stay put for a moment. Grab the opportunity to speak to him while I can.

'Sioe da!' I say, enthusiastically.

He smiles. 'Diolch. I don't know if people got it, actually. It was supposed to be a comedy. Didn't hear much laughing.'

'It was funny. But it was profound too.'

And he nods, a knowing but grateful nod.

My belly flips as I stand there. Giddy with the smell of him. I know it's naïve to think he's interested, because I know he hasn't texted. Only I can't help but feel that he's chuffed to see me too. And that there's still a chance. I mean, there's definitely still a connection.

'Sori. That I haven't been in touch.'

'It's fine. You've been busy, 'aven't you?'

Just then, another parent congratulates him. He touches my arm lightly.

'Catch you again, yeah?' And he turns away.

♥

It was after finishing my white wine that it happened. Gwen was fast asleep after the concert, and I was sat on the sofa watching some crap programme about cruises.

A knock at the door.

And I mean, I hate to say it, but I *knew* it was him this time. I mean, Richard had only just left and no one else would be calling at this time of night. It was a post Christmas concert booty call. And I was chuffed to bits.

I remember taking a deep breath before opening the door. Tryin' to make my eyes look bright.

Only it wasn't him standing there. It wasn't him at all.

Good Pals

She's lookin' gaunt in the face. The little ones are asleep. One in the pushchair, and Perry on her chest.

'Don't say it, I can't be arsed.'

'I wasn't goin' to say nothin'.'

'A cup of tea, that's all I need.'

I drag her heavy suitcase into the flat.

She carries Carly and Perry onto the sofa. We put a blanket over them. Tuck them in.

Then I take her into my bedroom and go make a cup of tea. When I come back, she's sitting on the duvet staring at her hands.

'So what have you been up to, then?'

And I smile, because that's a very important thing to remember about an asker of questions. They seem to understand that you can hide in other people's lives for a while if you ask things.

That night we share my bed. It feels strange, having another woman in bed with me. Especially Arse. We probably haven't done it since we were eighteen. Before we had kids. Before the world started growing up around us.

We're both in our nighties. Both bare-legged. And truth be told, I think we're both excited. Even during the shittiest of times, it's sometimes possible to feel a strange sense of wellbeing when you share a bed with a friend.

Because tonight, like the kids in *The Lion, the Witch and the Wardrobe* as they hide from the the White Witch in Narnia, all we have to do is make it through one dark night until morning. And there's a comfort to be found in that. A feeling that yesterday and tomorrow can't touch us. At times like these, the only thing you can have faith in is the present. And perhaps that isn't such a bad thing.

'I had sex last week …' I say, all mischievous. Knowing full well that she's going to be wide awake with intrigue.

'You had wha'?'

I laugh. 'Cos she has got comic timing, fair play.

'With the deputy head of Gwen's school.'

She turns in bed, folds the pillow in two and comes closer. I can tell that she's completely confused, and slightly annoyed that I haven't texted her about it.

'The sexy one? Fuck me, Sam!'

'No, actually. Fuck me.' She giggles like mad then, kicks one leg out of the duvet because she's too warm. I've left the heating on for them. Payin' through my nose for it too.

'What's his cock like?' And the old Arse comes out to shine. Just like she was in school. Crude and incredible. Getting away with it because of the sweetness of her voice and because she's being ever so slightly ironic. At least, I hope she is.

'It's him who's put that post-it thingy on the door then, is it?'

'What?'

'There's some note on the door. Thought it might be Richard, stalkin' you again.'

Without a moment's hesitation I get out of bed, all sheets and feet, and stumble through the dark.

When I open the door and see it, I know I was right to keep hoping.

One bright pink post-it note, stuck to the outside of the front door. Flicking out like a tongue.

I grab it. Read it.

Ti'n seren

Welsh for *You're a star*, and I can't catch my breath for the excitement of it. I consider texting him, but the romance of this little note says it all. Maybe he wants to woo me like they used to do in the old times. Throw stones at my window. Step out with me. Take me to the fair when it comes to Ponty. Kiss me behind the dodgems …

I twirl with the fun of it, and my nightie becomes a bright fuschia ball gown. On top of the world, I waltz back to the bedroom. Feel so special, it's unreal.

I whisper in the dark as I bounce into bed. 'Oh my God, you got to see this!'

Only she doesn't answer. Because she's fast asleep and far away. And I'm glad for her.

Bonnie Lass

'No one open their eyes!'

It's a cold, crisp night and we're all standing on the roof of the flats. No one much knows about up here. No one much cares either.

'Can I open them now?' Gwen's peeking through her fingers.

'No peeking, Gweni!' and she shrieks with laughter.

'Come on, mun,' Arse is more impatient than the children. 'I'm freezin'.'

And so finally, I let them, shouting 'Nadolig Llawen!' as they open their eyes. I've only had half an hour to prepare, but I've managed to light four lanterns and put out three plastic chairs. And all around us, Pontypridd is shining her lights.

'I've got tea in a flask!' I show them. 'Mince pies. And music!' and I switch the radio on.

'It's amazin' up here,' Arse says enthusiastically.

'I have a sneaky fag up here sometimes when her-by-there have gone to bed. It's a good place to see the fireworks too.'

'We gonna have a disco on the ceiling?' Gwen asks.

'Roof. You have a disco on the *roof*, not on the ceiling.' Arse laughs.

'Well, we've got the music already haven't we,' I suggest, 'so let's just have a boogie!' and Gwen's away.

Twirling excitedly. Laughing and screaming and getting a tad hysterical.

'Tea for us grown-ups,' I say, whispering the rest of the sentence in Arse's ear, 'with brandy in it. Let's celebrate the fact that I'm unemployed.' Arse gives me a look. Sad but a little amused.

As the Pontypridd lights smudge pleasantly into the background, we sit back and let the kids play. There are colours everywhere you look tonight. Christmas lights shining. Orange stains, exotic blues, red smudge marks like lipstick on a mirror and then the white of the A470 lights. White like the laces on new trainers. It's as good as it can get really.

I pass Arse a plastic cup full of brantea (as I end up callin' it). Bein' the genius that I am.

'Alan called today,' she says then, and suddenly I feel as sober as a saint. 'I told him we're not comin' home for Christmas.'

I'm so proud of her. That she's beginnin' to see sense. Only I don't say anything. I just drink my tea. Hot tongue tea. Zinging with whispers of brandy.

'Pass me a mince pie, will you?' she asks then to lighten the mood. So I do.

'Oh my god, they're warm! Did you *make* these?'

'Nope. Mam and Peg did. Stopped 'em from killing each other up the house this afternoon. I'll have to think of something else to stop them tomorrow.'

'So, have you texted that Arwyn bloke yet?' Arse asks, munching away at her mince pie.

I shake my head, smug with my own self-control, 'I'm gonna. Straight after Christmas.'

'How come nothin' that romantic have ever happened to me?' I smile. Feel a bit guilty.

We don't talk about anything important after that. Just gossip, giggle and sit on the roof pretendin' we rule the world. Well, Pontypridd at least. I don't tell Arse, but I've managed to pinpoint Arwyn's flat from up here too. Which is a nice feeling. And even though I really shouldn't, I can't help but wonder what's around the corner. And whether he'll be standing here with me. On this roof. Next year.

You and I

I called Harry on his mobile this morning. To tell him that Peg was back from her travels. He sounded shocked to begin with. Then excited.

After the call, I went and had a lie down on my bed. Truth be told I just wanted to read through the post-it notes that were still appearin' on the front door. Pink, green, blue and fluorescent yellow. Still dazzlin' me.

It was Mam's message that snapped me out of it first.

LOVE. GoOD newS. Gareth's not doing the Irak interview no more. LOL. Text back. XXX

But the second disturbance was a knock on the door.

When I first clapped my eyes on her, I couldn't quite place her. Truth be told, I don't know if I'd ever seen her outside the café before.

'Pauline.'

'Wanted to bring you this.' She handed me a tiny Christmas card. One of those cards that are so small it's bloody pointless that they even exist. I wasn't sure what to say to her. It was as if without the café in common, I didn't really know her at all.

'How's Carol?'

'Apparently, she's 'elpin' 'er sister with the all day breakfast van up the Beacons.'

I nodded.

'And how's …' I couldn't remember her husband's name. I felt so bad.

'He's fine,' she said scrunching her little cupid mouth to the side. 'I've been thinkin' a bit actually, since I last saw you. 'Cos I read this thing in the *Western Mail*, see. About John Lewis. And about the fact that the miners built the welfare hall.'

Suddenly, and so unexpectedly, Pauline began to look like hope. Even her small cupid mouth and her perfectly filed nails.

'D'you fancy a cuppa? I've got some mince pies we could have.'

But Pauline shook her head. Nervous like a bird again.

'Best not. Need to do my shoppin' before I catch the bus back.'

And off she went then. Just like that. Leaving me on my own doorstep. Christmas twinklin' in my toes.

'I'll phone you is it? In the New Year?' I shouted as she disappeared around the bend.

'Yeah,' she said shyly before shufflin' away. Apologising to the floor for treading on it.

♥

I love the normality Arse brings to the flat. In fact, I don't know what I'll do when she's gone. Tonight we've settled down to watch a repeat of Jamie Oliver in Marrakesh. We're sippin' from mugs of tea and Arse has put her legs up on the sofa. She's really small and can tuck herself into places like I can't. Not that I'm hellish tall or nothin', but I'm more gangly somehow.

Towards the end of the programme, Jamie goes to this market and loads of the men who work there recognise him. They've seen him on telly. All the way over in Africa.

'Bish bash bosh,' says one of the boys and they all laugh. 'I'm the only gay in the village,' says another. Jamie looks mega chuffed, and Arse laughs. 'That's bloody amazin', that is. That they know that! And that gay in the village thing is from Wales!'

I laugh too, only I don't feel like laughin'. Because, truth be told, it makes me a bit sad. Like as if the world has become too small. Those boys in Marrakesh, they shouldn't know lines like that. They should have their own shit to laugh about.

'I reckon he's gonna ask you out again before Christmas,' and as she says it, a glorious nervousness grows inside of me. The way he's wrapped me round his little finger. The way she's brought this up like a bolt from out of the blue.

'He is pretty romantic, I'll give him that,' I say, trying not to show how excited I am about everything.

Then we both just watch telly again, feeling like two little girls whose Mams are drinking tea out of a teapot in the kitchen. Only we are the Mams. And I haven't even got a teapot.

KEEP COOL

Christmas Eve has come again, and the smell of Christmas is all around us. I can't put my finger on what it is. That familiar smell. Attic dust on the tinsel. Sofa smells on your clothes. Someone else's fart up your nose.

Gwen is in the window and I'm sitting on the sofa with Mam and fat-man-Terry. Mam's bought the *Radio Times* for once, bein' as it's a special occasion, and we're watchin' this Welsh programme about this place called Bethlehem in west Wales. Fat-man-Terry and Mam are reading the subtitles, and I'm the only one able to get the lingo. And Gwen, of course, but she's not interested. She's more interested in looking out for Santa. Which is fair enough if you ask me.

Her voice slides out from behind the curtains.

'Do Siôn Corn come in through the door?'

'Yes, love, he *does*.'

'Why?'

I look at Mam and roll my eyes.

''Cos he can't come down the chimney because there isn't one,' I explain.

'Is it?' she asks. 'Or is it 'cos he've got a belly like Terry?'

I don't look at Terry. Just keep my eyes fixed on the telly.

'Do Siôn Corn know to take Carly and Perry and Arse's presents up the flat now?'

And it's Mam's turn to roll her eyes this time. At me. 'You don't call her *Arse* in front of the kids, do you?' and I just concentrate on watching telly, as if this programme is the best and most interesting thing I've ever seen. I don't take well to people tellin' me how to raise my own child. Especially my own Mam.

'Do Siôn Corn speak Welsh *and* English?' The curtains twitch as she moves.

'I reckon he speaks all the lingos,' fat-man-Terry says, with an unnaturally considered answer.

'Pass me the Celebrations, will you?' Terry asks then, and I chuck him over the ones I don't like.

I look at Mam, and notice that she's made a real effort. Eyeshadow all carefully brushed onto her eyelids. Peach blusher stuff all over her cheeks.

'You look nice, Mam,' she snorts as if she wouldn't believe it even if Brad Pitt said it to her. 'Well, you do. So deal with it.'

Bored, I head over towards the curtains. Decide to look out at the night sky with my daughter. There's something different about being between the window and the curtains. Something otherworldly.

'Where's Peg?' I shout, hoping for an answer from Mam.

'Gone for a little nap, she has. Wants us to wake her for ·when Mass comes on telly.' Mam has a brightness to her voice now. As if she's suddenly accepted that she might be looking good.

Gwen snuggles up to me, 'Is Daddy with Bampy Ton?'

182

'Aye. But he's coming Christmas Day, remember. With more presents from Siôn Corn.' Gwen smiles. 'Gareth and Anj are coming over too,' only she doesn't smile at this.

'Tawel now!' Gwen demands after a while. 'You can't look for Siôn Corn and make a *noise*. You've got to try and look with quiet. Wait for Rudolph.'

'Ti'n gweld e?' I test her.

And then suddenly, she's sure she's seen something darting through the air.

'I seen it! I seen it!' she shrieks and her body goes into little spasms. She ducks under the curtains, just managing to avoid banging into the three-piece suite.

'Careful,' I bellow.

'Bampy Terry!' she screams as I remain behind the curtains looking up at the sky, 'Bampy Terry, I seen him! And his sleigh!'

Terry laughs heartily and makes my toes curl up. As I lower my eyes to the garden path, I clock him. Heading towards the front door. Richard. Without drawing attention to myself, I get up before he gets a chance to ring the bell. There's no way he's coming in.

Suddenly, I'm standing out in the cold.

'What you doin' here?'

'I was passin', so I thought I'd say Nadolig Llawen. Is Gwen still up?'

'No. She's sleepin'.'

And even though he's a bastard, and even though he reminds me of all the things I'll never become, and all the things we'll never be together, I can't help but feel like we're equals. As if we're from the same world.

'Hope you're havin' a nice night,' he tries his hardest, only I just don't let his words get through my skin.

He moves his feet in the cold. Doesn't know what to say next.

'Better go. Got a gig at nine.'

'On Christmas Eve?'

'Aye, yeah,' he says, 'we've been playin' loads recently. Done some gigs down Cardiff and in Aberdare.'

'You didn't tell me.'

'You didn't ask,' and he tries to pull back from the argument. 'It's all getting back on track, Sami. And Chief's mate Barber reckons he might have some odd jobs for me come the New Year too.'

'Believe that when I see it.'

I rest my hand on the front door, ready to close it. He's not thick. He can tell that I want him gone. And soon, he has. And I'm glad.

'What you doin' in the dark, Mam?'

I stand there for a moment. Not sure what to say.

'Making sure that Siôn Corn will be able to come through the door okay,' I explain, with excitement dusted over my words.

'Mam,' she whispers, 'come an' look by here!' She takes my hand and sneaks towards the lounge door with me in tow.

I can see that fat-man-Terry has his annoying arm around Mam, and that they're kissing. I want to puke, but

I don't think Gwen wants to. She's intrigued, by the looks of it. She's intrigued by the happiness of it. She hasn't seen that a lot recently. Not in our flat, at least. Just then she issues a tremendous giggle, with the sole purpose of being caught out. Terry pulls back from Mam, and they both laugh.

'Where's that little girl?' he asks accusingly and she wriggles and squeals like a piglet behind the door, excited by the whole prospect of being chased around the house.

'Did you hear that now?' Terry asks Mam, and she agrees with a nod. 'Well, I'm gonna 'ave to go and see what's making that noise. If it's not a little girl, then what is it? Eh? A monster?' Gwen shrieks and starts bounding up the stairs. Fat-man-Terry pounces from the sofa and runs after her, winking at me on the way. Only he's out of breath before he even starts. As pathetic as an old dog.

'Don't wind her up, d'you hear me? I want her asleep within the hour.' He does an annoying thumbs-up then. His belly flopping over his jeans, stretching his bottle-green T-shirt as far as it can stretch. For a while then, it's just me and Mam. On the sofa. Like the olden times.

'Is Gwen gonna come to something?' I ask then, because the thing is, bollocks aside, I can tell that she's bright like me. Only nothing much have come of me, so why the hell would anything much come of her.

''Course she is. She's gonna go to uni,' Mam says, with a sadness in her eyes. Because that's exactly what everyone said about me until I left school after my GCSEs.

Terry re-enters the room. 'She's in her pj's waiting for you.' I want to scream at him for helping, because Richard should be the one doin' that.

'Wake Peg up on ewer way down, will ew, love?' Mam says, as I head upstairs. 'She'll kill me if she doesn't get her eggnog on Christmas Eve.'

I try to speak in hushed tones as I tuck her in. Warn her about waking up in the middle of the night. Try to smile enough too. Only because I know that this is all a part of her map.

I mean, we've all got a map in the back of our heads. It's like our default. The things we know to be true. And I know that the things I'm saying tonight, especially *tonight*, are being soaked up like a sponge. At her age, on Christmas Eve. I mean, this is blueprint stuff. These things are going into her wiring. Deep into her forever. That's why I think Christmas doesn't feel as Christmassy once you're an adult. It's because you've got your map. Full stop. Done.

'D'you think Siôn Corn will remember to bring the Magic Tree?' and as she asks, I can feel beads of sweat forming on my forehead as if they've been waiting for this very moment.

'What was that now?'

'I sent him another letter in school.'

'What did it ask for?'

'The Magic Tree. Like Eylsa's having. And I said I wanted the house to be made of chocolate when I wake up on Christmas Day too.'

I ignore the whole thing about the chocolate house. I don't tend to acknowledge that I've heard things like that. Ever.

'Thing is,' I pull the duvet around her tightly, 'letters you send from school don't always get to Siôn Corn see. Not in time anyway. So we might have a problem.'

'No, but it's okay, I think,' her lids are heavy with sleep now, 'because he said he'd try his best to get them.'

'You spoke to Siôn Corn then, did you?'

'Yeah, so don't worry, Mam. He said he'll sort it all out.'

And I love the fact that she's in this little world. A place where it all makes sense. I sit there for a while as she drifts away. Try to soak in the Christmas she's living. Try to catch the essence of it. The fun of it. The strength of belief. And for a moment, I think I've captured it; that old feeling of knowing that there's something more than you.

Sitting there on her bed, I can kind of imagine that Siôn Corn is doin' his rounds now and that he actually does exist. And then, I lose grasp of it again and the feeling slips away, like when you try and remember last night's dream.

As I leave the little bedroom Mam has made up for her especially, I kind of see how believing in God is the same as believing in Santa in a way. I mean, knowing that we're not the beginning and the end of it. That's what it's all about in the end. Knowing that we're just a part of something bigger and that there are some things we'll never understand.

A groggy Peg comes downstairs with me, focused on one thing only. Her Christmas drink.

'Pass me the eggnog, pass me the bloody eggnog.'

'D'you want eggnog, do you, Peg?' Mam closes one eye, looks like a pirate.

Terry's gone up the Legion for a pint with his mates and us girls are left by here. Watchin' Peg get woozy. We sit in silence for a while. Mam reading the *Radio Times* with her glasses on, and me and Peg watching telly. Three pairs of knees, knocking against each other on Mam's tiny sofa.

'Harry and me been planning while you've been away. Your big meet up in January.'

I watch her watching me. Wondering what I know. Wondering what he's said. Only I don't let on. I don't let on that I know anything.

'You know I loved him, don't you,' she says then, clutching onto her eggnog. Her blue eyes are nearly translucent now. Mam listens in, even though she's pretending to read the *Radio Times*.

'He *got* me.'

'Well maybe I shouldn't be with you when you meet up then,' I say playfully, 'in case you want to have rampant sex.' Mam throws me a look, but worse still, Peg doesn't laugh back. She just smiles sweetly, and lowers her head.

'He didn't see it like that,' she stares into her eggnog. 'I don't think he ever wanted to hold my hand, even.'

Mam looks up from the *Radio Times*. No way of hiding that she's been listening.

'Life's funny sometimes,' Mam says gently, 'gets all out of sync.' Only Peg doesn't look up. I'm convinced by now that she's crying, so I lean towards her and spot that she's fast asleep.

'Out for the count,' I say to Mam and she rolls her eyes.

'Pissed as a fart too.'

'Sad, though. What she just said.' Mam throws her head back. 'Who knows what's true with her.'

'She's telling the truth about this,' I say then, taking the eggnog out of Peg's hand. And that's when Mam decides to throw her curveball.

'When were you plannin' on tellin' me, then?' And she looks at my belly.

I screw up my face. Annoyed with what she's tryin' to imply.

'Get off. I'm not pregnant!'

Only that's when it hits me like a train. That I could be. And that I might have known, deep down, all along.

Mam reaches for the eggnog, unscrews the top and takes a gulp directly from the bottle. 'Don't tell Peg I did that.'

Then she draws the curtains, and doesn't say anything more about it. No more about the fact that there could be a baby inside me. No more about nothing.

'We better get this one upstairs,' she says eventually, looking at Peg slumped on the sofa, her mouth open. 'Dread to think what she's dreamin' about.' Only I have a fair idea. I reckon he lives down Rhiwbina. And has a hearing aid.

♥

Lying in bed that night, I forget that it's even Christmas Eve. There's no way around it any more. I'm expecting another baby. It had crossed my mind at least twice in the past fortnight. A pain in my back. A nauseous feeling in the morning. Only it could have been anything. And that's what I'd told myself every time the thought crept into my mind.

I should be lying here smiling now. Hoping. Thinking about our future. But I'm not. I have no one to blame but myself for this. I was the one who let him in. I was the one who decided to sleep with him. Yes, I was careful, but not as careful as I should have been. The most careful thing to do would have been to leave him at the door. Tell him to get lost.

And then I cry. Quietly. For this baby inside my belly, who has nothing at all to do with this mess. And who will be loved. And cherished. Just like Gwen.

THINK PINK

'I got a karaoke machiiiiiiiiiiiiiiiiiiiiiiiine!' And she's off again. We've all been dragged out of bed, half asleep, nodding and occasionally clapping. Peg is still fast asleep, nursing a huge hangover. Mam, on the other hand, is wide awake, as she's been up since six putting the turkey in the oven.

'And Siôn Corn remembered the magic treeeeeeeeeeeeeeeeeeee!' she screams, before throwing it to one side. I sit there for a moment, wondering where the hell it came from. Just then, Terry throws me back a wink. I'd love to frown at him, but I decide to accept it gracefully. Deep down, I know he's only tryin' his best.

'I heard him in the night! I knew he'd come,' Gwen says, in her little purple dressing gown and Disney slippers. 'He shouted Merry Christmas to a man on the street and I heard him fall over on the way into the house.'

I glance towards a sheepish Terry.

By half-past eight in the morning, Christmas Day presents are all but over. Now all that remains is that long and sleepy period until lunchtime, when everyone sits in the lounge helpin' Gwen put batteries in the back of things with cartoons on mute while Mam slaves away in the kitchen.

I give Arse a quick ring in the flat, and she tells me

they're fine. She says they're going to call with her Mam later on. Then I think about Harry. Hope he's okay. And then I think about Arwyn. I've been wondering about him all morning, truth be told. What he's up to. How he celebrates Christmas Day. Whether they all talk Welsh to each other all day. Whether he's thought about me at all.

Mam calls me into the kitchen after a while. Says she wants me to help her with the vegetables. Even though the turkey's nearly ready, she's left the veg a bit late, which probably means that everyone will be seriously tipsy by the time we sit down to eat. Great, I think to myself. Can't wait for that one.

♥

The moment he arrives, I'm annoyed with him. Truth is, he only has to breathe to get on my nerves.

'Daddy! Come an' see my prezzies!'

He follows her, nodding a 'hello' at fat-man-Terry, who's busy munching on a selection pack.

'Alright mate?'

'Aye.'

Peg looks up just as Richard passes her a box of Milk Tray.

'Got you these, Peg. Not diabetic are you?'

'No,' she says, snatching them from him, 'only on the weekends. In fact, these'll do great for the New Year's pensioners' raffle.' She beams a toothy smile and he laughs. He's always loved the cheek of her.

By now, Gwen is playin' house on the carpet. Piling her presents up in a tidy heap.

'Bampy Terry got me that. Lovely present,' she informs him knowingly, as if she was a grown woman.

Richard grabs a colourful skippin' rope, which she snatches from his grasp.

'Nooo! That's for later, for me to show you.'

I get hellish mixed feelings in that moment. I'm still annoyed by the fact that he's here, only I can't deny the fact that Gwen is so happy.

'Where's ewer presents from Siôn Corn for me?' she asks then, her hair in her face, fussy fingers all over her new things.

'Ah. Now that would be tellin'.'

She laughs and rolls about.

'Watch that new mug now,' I say as she continues to roll. A proper little show-off. Richard turns towards me then. He's been biding his time, I can tell.

'You look nice.'

'Don't know why the hell that would be. I haven't even washed my face.'

Little Gwen looks up at me, disappointed, and Peg makes herself look busy by reading through the *Radio Times*.

'Daddy,' Gwen says then, wanting to be the centre of attention. 'I wanna sing for you now. Do you a show.' Richard smiles then. I swear, he nearly looks handsome. Only it doesn't last long.

Gwen struggles to her feet, brushes her blond hair

from her face and puts one hand on her hip. Then, as if she's been practising all day, she points towards the karaoke machine in the style of a world class singer.

'Now which song d'you want me to sing? 'Cos I've got millions.'

♥

'Never liked sprouts,' Peg throws one over towards Gareth, laughing. It lands in his lap. Warm and small.

'No prankin' about now, Peg,' Mam says as she passes slices of turkey around with a proud glow in her cheeks. We all start piling our plates high and Terry starts tuckin' in. Only as he does so, Gareth coughs.

'I'd like us to say grace.'

Mam nods. She's all for the extra trimmings at Christmas.

'*I* want to do it!' Gwen's blue cracker hat falls from the top of her head, ending up around her neck. 'We do do it in school.'

We all lower our heads.

'Gweddïwn,' Gwen declares, and everyone takes a quick look up at each other, amused that it's gonna be in Welsh. She catches sight of our white eyeballs. 'Gweddïwn, I said!' And we all duck down again. Scared for our lives.

'O Dad yn deu ludedwydd y dewuna diolcho'r new cansoth lawy dawbob dydd ein chluniaeffa'n chlawenyf. AMEN!'

And we all clap, which is insane! Because we should be sayin' amen after her. But we're so proud of her for speaking Welsh that we forget what we're up to. Anj, on the other hand, looks a little disgruntled.

'What about if Anj says one too, in English?' I say then.

After all, I was the only one who knew that Gwen's prayer had only *just* made sense in Welsh. Anj lowers her head.

'For what we are about to receive, may the Lord make us truly thankful.'

Gwen shouts an abrupt 'AMEN!', as if she's annoyed she's been upstaged.

We all stuff ourselves from then on. Sticking pieces of things in our mouths we don't usually taste. The brown meat from the turkey. The bitterness of the sprouts. The squidgy bread sauce on our tongue. All our shoes touching because the table's too small to sit us all comfortably.

'You've put on a feast, mun!' Terry says, with pieces of stringy turkey hangin' from his fork. I notice he haven't got too much on his plate. Probably because he's going to do exactly the same thing in about an hour. With his ex-wife.

'I told my friends in my class my Dad is a pop star,' and Richard smiles like the cat who got the cream. Hairs coming from his nostrils. Big broad shoulders on a slim frame.

After a while, Peg gets up from the table and excuses herself. Says she'd rather let what she's eaten settle, rather than pile more on top of it. Truth be told, I think Gareth and Anj just get on her nerves.

'Always do a lovely roast dinner you do, Janet. Fair play to you,' Richard says to my Mam. She smiles at him, chuffed. He's always been ever so perfect when he needs to be.

♥

Leavin' the others to chat about flames on Christmas puddings, I head for the living room. I'd rather sit with Peg and listen to her bollocks than listen to Richard spoutin' off all afternoon.

She's sat on the sofa when I come in. Legs crossed, face towards the telly. Looking ever so ladylike.

'Don't blame you for comin' out here,' I say then, 'they're all a bunch of nutters.'

Only she doesn't answer me.

I head towards her and notice that she's sleeping. Only she looks different, somehow. I don't know what it is that tells me that something's up. It happened with Nanna too. It's as if you can sense the fact that they've left the building. Gone. Back to wherever the hell we've all come from. How can you possibly disappear like a shootin' star in the dead of night when you were as alive as Peg? How can that possibly be?

The final breath comes so suddenly in the end, I realise. Abruptly. In silence.

♥

It's a bit like giving birth, is grief. They say you forget how much it hurts because of the jubilation you feel when the baby lies on your belly. All wet and wild. I reckon it's the same with death and hurt and mourning. You forget about the periods of numbness, the periods of weirdness. You choose not to remember.

I sit there with her body under a Mickey Mouse duvet cover for the rest of the evening. She's so small, you can only just make out that she's there. I don't mind it, to be honest. Keepin' her company. I did the same with Nanna. I mean, what difference does it make if she's dead or alive? Actually, she's probably less trouble now she's dead. Havin' said that, I wouldn't put anything past Peg.

Fat-man-Terry is still with his ex-wife, so I tell Mam to go to bed. Tell her I'll stay with Peg until the funeral directors come. Mam's strugglin' to catch her breath for tears as she heads upstairs, only for some reason, I don't have cryin' in me now. The only thing I have is a feelin' that I can't leave Peg on her own.

Sittin' there, all those feelings come flooding back. How it felt when Nanna died. How it felt when Dad got locked up. Then that strange feelin'. A feelin' as if life is short and long and strange.

At that moment I become highly aware of the fact that there's a baby too. Sitting in my belly. And that Peg didn't even know. There's life and death all around me tonight. Growing and dying. The beginning and the end, and the wonder of it all, melting together until I don't know which one comes first anymore.

I'm in a world of my own when she comes in. Her eyes full of sleep.

'What you doin' down? It's late.'

I get up and move away from Peg.

'I want hot water bottle. My feets are cold.'

'Alright. Mam do it now. You go and tuck yourself in.'

She points over towards the Mickey Mouse duvet cover. Concern on her face.

'What's Peg doin'?'

'Sleepin', love.'

Gwen just stares for a moment, wonders to herself.

'Why don't you just say she's dead, like on television?'

'Okay,' I say quietly, 'Peg's dead.'

'Tell ew what,' she says then, 'let's do her a hot water bottle too. Case her feets are cold.'

I look at my little girl with a lump in my throat. Her glossy blond hair glistening in the livin' room light. As wise as an old barn owl and as oblivious as a dormouse.

♥

After about an hour of sitting on my own in the dark, I hear the gentlest of knocks on the door. A knock that's so damn considerate it makes me want to scream. Goes right through me, does people tryin' to be too 'sensitive'. There's just no need for it.

Before I answer the door, I decide to take one last look at Peg. Once they come in, she'll be gone. Taken away by strangers and treated like any other dead body that rocks up at the morgue. Only she's not just anybody. She's Peg.

I pull back the Mickey Mouse duvet cover and look at her. Hair-sprayed, dyed, blue-black hair. Bright green eyeshadow on wrinkly, mottled skin. Pencilled-on eyebrows and a heart of gold. There's no mistaking it. That soul sure left a mark on that body. And that's how it should be.

There's a knock on the door again. Louder this time.

And then just like that, a softly-spoken man pussyfoots around the house and manages to make Peg disappear. Just like a magician. I mean, I don't even remember them moving the body. It's as if they came in and cast a spell.

I stand by the window. Watch the black hearse glide smoothly along the street. Suddenly, my heart really pumps with the hurt of it. It's as if the emotional dial has switched from zero to max in the space of a second. My aunty, I think to myself. Leavin' the house for the last time. Just like my Nanna did. And for a moment it dawns on me that I don't quite know what this world is going to be like without them both. These people who frame my world.

Just as I'm about to draw the curtains on the night, something catches my eye. Now, I know that Arse will say that I was hallucinating because of grief, but I swear that what I see is as real as my own pulse.

Walking up the road, with their backs to me, I see two old ladies. One is small and crooked and the other has a mop of white hair on her head. They're in a world of their own. Chattin' away. And they're definitely there. Peg and Nanna. Reunited at last. Suddenly, I get this urge to be with them. Not in a suicidal way or nothin'. Only there's a warm glow about them. As if they've finally arrived somewhere we'd all like to be one day.

And in that moment, I can't help but feel as if I've been left behind. In a mess, with a baby in my belly.

HEART'S DESIRE

It's a few days after New Year's Day that Harry comes up to Ponty in the car to see me. Says he'd like to go for a drive. I think it's because I'm the only person he can grieve with. And that's fine by me.

He told me on the phone that he wouldn't be coming to the funeral, only I didn't ask why. I didn't feel it was my business to ask. It was bad enough havin' to tell him that she'd passed away.

These last few days have been rough. Peg's funeral hanging over us all like some dead dog. I can't help but feel a bit annoyed with her for dyin' so close to the New Year. It's a right old awkward time to try and arrange a funeral. And I'd tell her that to her face too. If only I got half a chance.

As soon as I've put my seatbelt on he tells me he fancies going up Eglwysilan. As we drive, I tell him that I've been findin' it hard to sleep. That I always end up thinking about Peg.

'Maybe you should just kid yourself that she's still in South America,' comes his reply.

'Be in denial, you mean?' And for a moment, I'm aware that I'm treading on thin ice. After all, it would be double denial, being as she didn't even go there in the friggin' first place.

'It's not denial, Sam. It's what people do. In fact, I've

been thinkin' a bit about that too. How glad I am that she got to see the world. Before passing away.'

I gulp. Concentrate on the road ahead. Just then, a thought strikes me. Maybe that's why Peg went away in the first place. Even if it was only to Bristol and the Rhondda Heritage Park Hotel. Maybe she was preparing us all for a day like today.

'I read something once,' his voice is sombre and steady, 'about time being a circle, and that everything actually exists simultaneously. I like that idea and I'm sticking to it. The idea that everyone I've lost is still alive. Existing, but just out of reach.'

Just then he turns on the radio and Classic FM flows around the car, filling my ears with violins. And I'm reminded of the fact that I used to listen to music like this back in the day. I'm glad to hear it today too, to be honest. He was gettin' a bit heavy for my likin', talkin' like that. 'Cos the problem with me is that heavy shit always sticks in my head. And then just goes round and round. Forever.

♥

'These post-it messages. They sound very sweet,' he says, as we head off from the pub car park in Eglwysilan. I can see that there are tens of people by the bar. Warm orange glows in the window. Us in the biting cold.

'Yeah well, he hasn't asked me out yet.'

As we walk, he pulls his collar up to shelter from the cold. I can see the hills in the distance. Greys and dark greens. A fresh New Year's feelin' suddenly bombarding my senses. Only it's tinged with confusion. Because things are bound to be different now that I'm expecting. The post-it notes feel faintly ridiculous.

Harry's quieter than usual today, and I don't like it. Sometimes I reckon I'd rather see someone lose their temper than swim inside themselves like Harry and Gareth can do. It really does unnerve me. And I'll tell you for why. It reminds me that at the end of the day, we're all alone inside our minds. No matter how much I like to think that all our thoughts are connected. No matter how much I like to believe that we're all one big person, wired up to each other by some invisible force. Sometimes we're really not.

Just then I feel my T-shirt riding up inside my coat. The cold of the air hitting my back. I'm going to have to get some new clothes when I can afford to. There's a beginning of a bump now. There's a change in shape. I haven't told Harry I'm pregnant. Seems odd, somehow, to have to say it out loud. And the strange thing is, I know I'll never tell him. Because I can't imagine we'll be seeing much of each other any more. We have no reason to.

We carry on walking, up a small path now, over towards a little hill. When we actually stop and stand and listen to the silence it nearly breaks my heart. It's too much like the truth is silence, sometimes. Forcin' me to remember that Peg's gone, and that this New Year might not be quite as perfect as I'd first hoped it might be.

Harry leads us over to an old wooden bench and we sit down. Look out at the view.

'Peg and I came up here once.'

'Did you?'

'Yes – I had to make a delivery, and she came with me.'

Harry reaches into his pocket and passes me something. I'm expecting a mint, only it's actually a little golden plaque. Winking brightly at me in the white winter light.

Peggy Lee Jones 1928–2013
Let your spirit roam free.

'I was thinking of getting it put on here.' He places his frail fingers on the back of the wooden bench. 'What d'you think? A bit cheesy?'

Before I get a chance to reply, a strong gust of wind comes from nowhere, rocking us both to our core. I smile at him through my hair. His eyes dazzle like diamonds. This flotsam and jetsam, I think to myself. This love of Peg's life.

Too Much

As soon as I'm up the stairs I spot it. The first post-it note of the New Year. Bright blue and glued onto the door of my flat.

Molly and the one remaining pup scramble around by the door as I enter. They're huffing, puffing and dribbling. Slipping about everywhere. Gwen dives in towards them and they lick her excitedly. I notice then that she's wearing a black patch on her left eye, tied around her head with elastic.

'Look at you.'

'Arse and me been playin' pirates!'

As she disappears back into the lounge, I read the message on the post-it note. It says *U Rock*. I smile before reaching into my pocket for my phone. Now that the New Year's settled in, it's surely time to meet up. I pause for a moment. Wonder whether I should bother, things being so complicated and all. But like an old wind, this feeling gusts over me. Of hope, of newness. Of downright naïve optimism.

Happy New Year Mr Pritchard! So when am I gonna see you in person then? ;) X

As soon as I finally send it, I realise it was a mistake. I mean, I haven't even told Richard about the baby yet.

I hear Arse's footsteps in the kitchen. Only the moment I step in there, I realise we have a visitor.

'When were you plannin' on tellin' me then?'

'I thought he knew,' she says then, screwing her face up awkwardly before disappearin' out of view.

'Is it mine?'

I look at him. Annoyed with the fact that he's even asked the question. My phone beeps. It's Arwyn.

Can I call over tomorrow night? X

I'm suddenly aware of how crazy my life is. How much of a mess it's become.

'Came over here to tell you I've got a job. Eighteen grand.'

'Isit?'

'Custards. Night manager.'

I smile a weak smile.

'Thought you'd be chuffed.'

'I am chuffed.'

'Finally growin' up, see,' only there's a desperation in him that makes me feel sad. Because I know that I've got my eye on better things.

'How do you fancy goin' down the ice rink in Cardiff? You, me and Gwen? I've seen adverts. It's still on for another weekend.' Before he even finishes his sentence I shake my head.

'We're busy this weekend.'

'I'll text you the details. 'Case you change your mind.'

'Fine,' I say then. Just to keep him happy. Only he knows that I won't shift. He knows me only too well.

'You're gonna have to learn to trust me again, mun,' he says then. Out of the blue. Like a ripple on the face of a stillwater lake.

'It's good about your job. Really good news.' Only he knows what I'm not sayin'. It's all there in the gaps between the words.

Moments later he's gone. Shuttin' the door quietly behind him.

After a breath, Arse returns. Big eyes. Awkward lips.

'I am so sorry. I thought you'd told him.'

As she puts the kettle to boil, I really begin to feel like two different people fightin' for the same skin. It's as if I'm totally out of control. I watch Arse prepare the tea. And truth be told, watching her is as much as my brain can deal with.

'I feel a bit weird,' I say to her. Feelin' vulnerable for even sayin' it. 'Like I can't handle everythin' as good as I can normally.'

'Tired, aren't you,' she says, passing me the tea, 'and still grievin'. For Peg. Don't be too hard on yourself.'

I nod. Sip my tea. Only her words feel too distant to make a difference.

♥

That night I lie wide awake in bed, with Arse by my side, snoring. I'm still not feeling myself, and in fact, I think

I'm feeling worse. It's as if the sky's fallen down on top of me over the past few weeks. One piece after another.

I decide to text Arwyn. Tell him to forget it. I grab my phone. Start typing.

I'm really sorry, but I can't meet up with you.

Only something stops me from pressing the send button. You can call it whatever you like. Survival. Denial. Hope. Desperation. But whatever it is, it's willing me on. Telling me it might just work out.

I Want U

It's three days before Peg's funeral, and I'm sitting in the flat with gorgeous skin, waiting for him.

I went to Boots first thing this morning and I've been exfoliating all day. Surprised I've got any skin left, to be honest. But anyway, point is, wherever he touches me, he'll glide. I've decided not to tell him that I'm pregnant. You can't tell yet, unless you know. At least, that's what I've convinced myself. I mean, it could just be a bloated belly bulge. Someone who's been eatin' too many carbs over Christmas.

Arse has agreed to take the kids over to her Mam's tonight. And I'm feelin' a little bit selfish for it. Only as soon as I've got myself ready, he's here. Knockin' at the door. I brush my palm against my cheeks once more to try and tone down the blusher. Then, I let him in.

'Helo, ti,' there's a cheeky smile smacked across his face, as if he's had a few pints. 'Glad I've got the right place.' I throw him an unbelieving look. After all, he's been delivering post-it notes for the last month or so.

'Took ewer time,' I say playfully, inviting him in and closing the door. He enters, and New Year air floods in like magic dust.

As soon as I get the chance, I press myself against him and kiss him on the lips. He reciprocates and moments later we're snogging against the wall. Telly programme style.

I go and fetch some beers then. Place a cold, dewy bottle in his warm hand.

'Good Christmas, 'te?' He nods. Explains in Welsh that his parents are barmy. I laugh. He's so funny. So naturally funny. I can't even believe I've managed to get him into this flat!

He says something else about presents then. How he hates them. And I laugh again, only I'm not really listening. I'm just looking at his hair. His eyelashes. He puts down his beer. Slides himself around me. Holds me and kisses me. A boozy concoction of beer and aftershave filling my senses. As he tries to put his hand up my top, I stop.

'Those messages,' I say, 'they were really cute.' He kisses me again.

'I try my best,' but he's reluctant to stop kissing.

'Was it because of the Love Hearts? Is that why you did the whole post-it note thing?'

He smiles, nods and kisses me again. Soon enough, without me even realising, I'm on top of him. This flotsam and jetsam. This new sun. I'm about to really let go when I hear someone come in through the front door. Shocked, I release myself from our tangle, and get up. I stand staring at Arwyn, my hair all over the shop. He looks at me, a question forming in his eyes.

'Don't know who it could be,' I say, confused. For a moment, I leave my gorgeous New Year catch in the lounge. Head for the hallway.

'Arse?' I shout as I walk. As soon as I turn into the kitchen, I come face to face with Richard.

'What you doin' here, mun?'

'Thought you were over Arse's Mam's with the kids,' he says, with a rabbit-in-the-headlights look about him.

He reaches down towards his feet. Grabs a Tesco bag.

'Thought I might get you and Gwen some things in. Thought maybe stuff with the funeral might be getting on top of you.'

He looks at my belly then. Without even tryin' to.

'You gave me a fright.'

'Sorry.'

'You shouldn't be here.'

He looks away.

'I want my keys back.'

And he immediately looks back at me. 'Cos what I've just said means everything. We stand there for a moment. Looking at each other. He reaches into his pocket and places the key on the table.

I hear a shuffle of feet. Arwyn's up off the sofa. Richard looks at me, notices the panic on my face. Arwyn's heading up the passage now. Please don't do this. Please don't.

He enters, smiling. Richard and Arwyn clock each other. Eyes first. Fixed eyes. Eyes, eyes, eyes. I gulp, feel my chest tightening.

'Richard. This is Arwyn.'

Richard doesn't even nod. He knows exactly who he is.

'Alright?' Arwyn smiles clumsily.

'I'm off,' says Richard then, marching towards the door.

I stand there looking at Arwyn. Listen to the front door being slammed shut.

'Who was that? Gwen's Dad?'

I nod.

'You're not still together, are you?'

I shake my head. 'He was just droppin' off some shopping,' And I indicate the bag. There's a strange silence before Arwyn grabs me, and pulls me against his taut belly.

In the embrace, and before we kiss again, I glance down at the bag. Spot a box of eggs. A loaf of bread. And a box of Milk Tray. Lying upside-down.

Arwyn kisses me, and it's at that moment that I clock it. The purple of the Milk Tray and something pink. Something pink lying on top of it. It's just like all the others. Sticking out like a tongue. Poking fun at me.

I release myself from Arwyn's gorgeous grasp.

'I thought you said you sent the messages,' I turn to face Arwyn.

'Huh?' Suddenly, he seems a little drunker. A little less attractive.

I step back from him. Size him up. This gorgeous creature I seem to have mistaken for someone else.

'What you even doin' here?'

'You're the one who sent me the message. Be sy'n bod arnot ti?'

I tie my hair back into a ponytail. Suddenly feel really pregnant.

'I think we've got our wires crossed here.' Only that's not really fair to say. Because I'm the only one who's crossed the wires.

He just stands there. Staring at me. A tiny hint in his eye that he thinks I'm off my head.

This flotsam and jetsam, I think to myself. This man I made from sea and sand, with the sheer will of my imagination. And I blush at the thought of it.

♥

Within a quarter of an hour, we're sitting together at the table drinking tea and eating toast, thanks to the loaf Richard brought over. It's all a bit awkward really, but he seems happy enough. Chompin' away.

They've disappeared like vapour in the sun. All those kisses. His hair on my face.

'I'm pregnant.' My statement sits with us at the table. Pulls up a chair. A thought bounces into his head, and I spot the exact moment it lands there.

'Don't worry. It was ages before you.'

Without noticing, he lets out a faint breath of relief. Ever so faint. But I notice. He asks me how Gwen is then. I say that she's fine, wonder how long we'll be able to sustain this banal conversation. After about five minutes, I want him gone, and if I'm being honest, I can tell that he wants the same.

Leading him to the front door, I smile a matey smile. I don't pout my lips. I don't wiggle my hips. I don't try to be beautiful anymore. I just act like me.

Bye-bye, flotsam and jetsam boy, I think to myself.

'Hwyl fawr, Sam,' he says, before heading down the steps, taking his language with him.

I sit in the kitchen after he's gone. Feeling like a fool. There are no distractions now. And the only thing I feel is fear. Deep down in my belly. Like an ache.

FEELING BLUE

I suppose it was a long time coming, really, but the day after flotsam and jetsam boy vanished into thin air, I just couldn't get out of bed. It was as if I was paralysed. All the energy zapped out of me. Arse thought I was poorly to start. Tried to get me to eat vegetables and yoghurt and stuff. Only I knew it wasn't a bug or an infection. I knew it was my brain. I felt exactly the same when I was fifteen and cutting into my arms. When Mam and Dad were arguin' like cat and dog. I was lost and out at sea.

This time, I stayed in bed for two whole days. Stared at the walls. Listened to the dogs bark durin' the night. Sometimes, I tried to make out faces and animals in the patterned material of the curtains. Other times, I drifted in and out of sleep. And when I finally managed a few hours, I would always dream about Peg. Wake up sweatin'. Then I'd be stuck there with my negative thoughts. Drivin' their way through my skull. Remindin' me of how shit I was and of how naïve I'd been.

Arse asked every day if I wanted to see Gwen. Only I didn't. She was better off staying at Mam and Terry's. Far away from all this crap.

Then, one night Arse came to sit with me. I could tell by the smell of her that she was going to try and 'talk' to me.

'I know it sounds mental,' I say then, the darkness hidin' my face. 'But I thought he might move in. That we'd all speak Welsh together.'

'You can speak Welsh with me,' she says, not meaning a word of it. And we laugh.

'You'd fuckin' laugh in my face.'

'Why are you so obsessed with speakin' Welsh anyway?'

'Piss off, isit?' I say, and we laugh again. Briefly.

♥

The night before Peg's funeral, fat-man-Terry and Mam come to see me. Terry sits at the bottom of the bed. Mam next to me, by my pillow.

'You've got to get up, love. It's doin' you no good.'

'I'm just depressed, aren't I.'

'I know, love,' she says, and she does know, because this is exactly what happens to her sometimes. 'But you'll regret it if you don't come to her funeral.'

I don't know how to answer. I want to be there. But my body feels so heavy. My mind blown apart.

'Try your best, love,' Terry says then, 'for Peg.'

His words grind on me. Buzz around my head like a swarm of bees. Only he doesn't stop there. 'Gwen's askin' after you all the time, in'she Carol?'

Mam nods.

'Bugger off Terry,' I bark. 'What you tryin' to do? Make me feel worse?'

'Don't talk to Terry like that,' Mam says then.

216

'Talk to him how I like. He's not my Dad.'

Terry sighs then, because we're back to this old chestnut. As if I'm a teenager again.

'D'you know how much Terry does for this family?'

Only I don't say a thing. And I don't intend to either. I just roll over, dragging a pillow over my head.

'Just get out my room,' I say, muffled under all the material.

And Terry does so. Straight away. Only Mam doesn't budge an inch, because she's never listened to me. She just sits there in the dark. Probably makin' out patterns in the curtain material.

'Heard about Richard's job,' she says after a few minutes of heavy silence, 'least he can support you now.'

'I don't want his support.'

'Can't you just try, Sam? He's said he's sorry.'

'I'm not gettin' back with him, Mam.'

'Yeah, well, maybe you should have thought about that before shaggin' him again. Me and Terry are only gettin' older.'

And with that, she's gone. Without even a good-bye.

♥

I weep for about twenty minutes after Mam's gone. And it's only when I stop cryin' that I notice that Arse is sittin' at the bottom of the bed.

'It's good you're gettin' it out,' she says eventually.

'I've got to get back with him, haven't I?'

'You don't *have* to do anything.'

217

'But he can take care of us.'

Arse comes closer and holds my hand. I look at her.

'I wouldn't even look at him if that Arwyn bloke was actually interested. That's how twisted this is.'

Arse sighs. Gives me the saddest look I've ever seen. It's nearly a look of disappointment. That I'm willin' to be so honest with the truth.

'Don't take him back if you don't want to.' She squeezes my hand. 'I've done it, haven't I?'

I sit up a bit.

'I'm not sayin' it'll be easy. But you don't *have* to do anything.'

'D'you think you could make me a Weetabix?' I ask then. 'Last thing I want to do is faint in this fuckin' funeral.'

BLESS YOU

'We're thinking of opening another bakery. Only not by here. In Taff's Well.' I watch Anj jabbering on. Notice that her black dress is too big for her. 'We're gonna call it Bread of Heaven 2. Bread of Heaven – Taff's Well.'

She looks so chuffed, I'm forced to smile.

'Taff's Well,' Terry says, 'but how are you?' and he laughs a belly laugh. Anj laughs too. It's as if they're on the same wavelength or something. In fact, I realise I haven't even seen Anj laugh before. I don't know whether I've ever seen her teeth.

'How do you fancy bein' the manager there?' she asks, and it takes me a second to realise what she's asking. 'Once it's open. I mean, you could catch a bus from Ponty and …'

'You serious? Brilliant!'

Mam's upstairs fussing. Pretending she's got nothing at all to do with what Anj has just said, only it's got her name written all over it.

Soon enough, both her and Gareth are standing at the bottom of the stairs, all bags and suits and hair done differently. Four vulnerable people in foreign clothes. Different smells and awkward looks. As if we've never really met before.

'Sam's up for the job,' Anj says, pushing Gareth out

the front door. Only Gareth doesn't react much really. Mam on the other hand, wants to know what Anj is talkin' about. Clever, that.

As we head for the car, I notice that it's a white sky day today. Not blue. Not grey. Just white and bright. Just like the day I went huntin' for Harry in the crem.

'Mam, mun, *I'll* go in the back,' Gareth stands outside the car in his white shirt and his black tie.

'No!' she fusses. 'You've got longer legs than me.'

I watch Mam lookin' at Gareth for a moment. Her face a little concerned.

'Got awful bags under ewer eyes, Gar.'

'Haven't been sleepin' too well, Mam,' he says abruptly before jumping into the car. As Anj drives away, we wave Terry and Gwen a goodbye.

'Excitin' about this job!' says Mam then, full of love and manipulation.

'Aye. Fancy that,' I say, feelin' like a puppet on a string.

♥

It was nothing like it was supposed to be. And that's what upset me. It was like a dry piece of toast with no butter on it.

Yeah, we sang, and the staff from the Home sang, and strangers sang, but nothin' out of the ordinary happened. Only it should have, because it was Peg's funeral. The boys from Porth football team, where Alf used to train the Under 21's, carried the coffin in, which was a bit bizarre. And Gareth. He helped carry it too. His face like stone.

Don't get me wrong, the preacher wasn't diabolical. I mean, he made it clear that Peg was no *average* spirit. Said things about her upbringing, which I'd mostly heard before. Then he said that Peg did a lot with the miners' strike, which reminded me of some stories I'd heard in the past. Those funny, fuzzy memories from your adolescence. When you weren't clever enough or wise enough to listen properly. We did laugh a bit too, about some of the stories he'd heard about her. But on the whole it was lackin' somethin'. Come to think of it, it was probably Peg.

It was towards the end of the ceremony that it came over me like an itchy rash you can't help but scratch. I wanted to stand up and say somethin'. I wanted to put on record how hellish special she was to me. Sitting there, I looked around at all the strangers' faces. Noses, chins and cheeks that I'd never seen put together before. It's a wonder you can get so many combinations really. And that's when it dawned on me that I'd be better off stayin' put. Because nothing I could say would bring her back.

♥

When I get back to the flat from the funeral tea, I come face to face with Arse, putting her coat on.

'Alright?' She looks embarrassed to see me.

'Thought you were goin' back to ewer Mam's.'

'Too tired. Just want to be on the sofa.'

And that's when I first see him. Alan. Heading back from the bathroom. He looks at me. Wonders how much I know.

'I'll take the cases down, Angharad,' he brushes past me without even a hello.

'You know how grateful I am, don't you? I don't know what I would've …'

And I just hug her. Hug her for the mistake she's making. She's still in the weather. The same old weather.

'How did it go today?' she asks then, typically tryin' to change the subject.

'Fine. Oh, I don't know. What you supposed to say about a funeral?'

She smiles at me. Carin' and tired.

'Ready?' Alan's voice comes from the hallway.

'I'll phone, yeah?' I nod, drying my tears.

'Come on then, Tinkerbell,' Alan says to Carly.

Arse looks at me for one final time before grabbing Perry and disappearing down the steps. I wave them all goodbye. Try and keep that fake smile glued to my face until they're gone.

On my own in the flat, I watch them from the window as they load the car. Tears drippin' down my face. From up by here they look like the perfect family. Packing the boot with things. Wrapped up in their winter coats. Ready to face the world. Only I know different. I know what's happening inside their heads.

As they get into the car, I secretly hope she's goin' to look up at me. She knows I'm by here waiting. She knows I'm looking down. Only she doesn't dare look back. And I don't hold it against her. Because she needs all the energy she has now, to look ahead. And battle on.

I HOPE

I'll never forget the words I woke up to.

The ring of my mobile. The early morning confusion. And Mam's voice. Mam's voice, wet with tears. Gareth. Tried to kill himself. Last night. After the funeral.

♥

I hate hospital smells. Anj says she does too. Mam's in with Gareth. So we just sit there. Us two. All fingers and thumbs. Heavy boots. Cardigans and jumpers that are too hot for over-heated hospitals. Our minds a mess.

'He has been struggling,' she looks down at the green floor, shining in the unrelentin' hospital light. Not letting anyone hide. Night or day.

'He's the kind who can cope in the day …' her voice is hoarse. She looks small and pathetic in her colourful jumper and skinny jeans.

I feel like shit for even thinking that everything was okay for him. That somehow, he'd been able to forget about all those things he's experienced. I feel bad for Anj too. Because I can tell she loves him. And I can tell that she's had to deal with those nightmares too. Unlike me, who just sees her brother in the daylight.

'They need to give him more counsellin',' she says then.

'It's gonna be alright,' I say, feeling myself slip into a role I've seen Mam play all my life. Truth is, I haven't got the faintest idea how things are goin' to be. But, somehow, you've always got to say it. And you've got to try and mean it.

'Where's Gwen to?' Anj seems to be genuinely wondering.

'Terry's taken her over to see his Dad.'

She just sits there then. Helpless. In silence. I mean, I wouldn't blame her for leaving. For running away from this doolally family. But I can tell, just like that-man-Terry, that she isn't going nowhere. And I respect her for it. Heck knows when and why anyone decides to make that decision, mind. That they're gonna stick around whatever happens. But she seems to have done it. Committed, in her head.

She looks over towards Gareth's ward.

'You're right, though, Sam,' she says, with a glimmer of hope in her voice. 'It is going to be alright. God's with him. He's been chosen.'

I head out for a breather after that, because I can't handle what she's talkin' about, and I don't want to argue with her at a time like this. I mean, she's got the right to believe whatever she wants, but as far as I'm concerned, if there is a God, he hasn't chosen Gareth any more than he's chosen me, Mam or Terry. God would choose everyone. The moment we come out of our Mams' bellies. And that's when I realise that I really believe in him or her. More than ever before. 'Cos to him, no one's more special than anyone else. He knows that we're all mental, and all special. Every damned one of us.

As soon as I go back in, a nurse appears from somewhere. She has such a tidy bob, it's unreal.

'Gareth,' she says, looking at us both, 'he'd like to see you.'

♥

'I've got a scan at two in the ward next door anyway. Good timin' really.' I kick my legs up onto the bed. Try and act as chilled out as I possibly can.

'Sam, mun!' Mam says. 'Get those shoes off those sheets,' so I do as I'm told.

Gareth's staring into nothingness. Me, Mam and Anj just lookin' at him.

'Look,' Mam says then, determined to fill the silence, 'we've all got to pull together on this one.'

Only the blowy silence continues. Starched sheets and big gaps between thoughts and speech. A silence that permeates through to my marrow.

'You don't need to feel guilty,' my voice echoes in this great big void. Because I reckon that's what he could be feeling. Heavy with guilt. 'You've done amazin', Gar, d'you hear me?' only Anj starts crying then. Deep, belly cryin', which is awful disturbing to hear.

'Can't push this under the carpet no more,' Mam says then.

Anj wipes her tears and holds Gareth's hand, only he's still not quite with us. Bloody hell, I think to myself, as I catch a look at us all on this hospital ward. How did we ever get to this point? Our little family. Doesn't seem like the place we were supposed to end up, somehow.

Finally, Gareth looks up. Speaks with a croaky voice, as if he has cut glass in his throat. 'I just didn't know how to stop it all.'

'I know,' Mam says then, clutching onto his fingers chaotically. Rubbing his palms with her thumbs. My heart could break in this room right now, I swear. What with this open-ended sky out the window, and with the way my Mam's rubbin' my brother's hand.

'I'm sorry,' Gareth doubles up then. Cries quietly without a sound.

Only as he cries, a tiny bit of hope begins to grow inside of me. It's as if my brain's reading between the lines. Ultimately, I don't reckon he wanted to die. He just didn't want to be so alone.

I look at Mam and Anj again. Their gaunt, pale faces. These lives, intertwined. Hope is what we need now, and plenty of it. And a pinch of Peg's attitude to life.

After he's finished cryin', it's as if he's back in the room with us. More awake somehow. Looking around, like a newborn baby who can't quite focus on anything. We settle into a different silence now. It's as if we're more at peace.

I gaze out of the window towards the trees and the white-bright sky that stretches on forever. I'm trying hard to think about the future as I look out. All of our futures. Our years to come. How would Peg see it? How would Peg survive it? I think about Gwen and that-man-Terry too, and I think about the little one growin' in my belly. And somehow, without even understanding where all this quiet hope is coming from, I begin to see tomorrow. Just past those trees. On that hill above town.

♥

That night, I sit in the reception area, waiting for Mam so that we can go home. I can't begin to imagine the pain she's been through over the years. Her little boy goin' to war, comin' back like he did. Destroyed. For a moment I feel hellish angry with the world. The people who sent my brother to war. A war he hardly even understood. And I wonder then, as I watch people comin' and goin', meetin' relatives, collectin' results, why we never seem to learn our lesson. Every generation makin' the same mistake as the one that's gone before, leavin' people shattered.

This weird feelin' washes over me then. A realisation that the people who are alive today are alone. 'Cos we always feel connected, don't we? Least I do, anyway. To all the people who've ever been on this planet. To everyone who has been before us. We feel like we're a part of a long, long everlastin' flow, from generation to generation. Only in a way we don't know nothin' except what we've lived. And the mistakes we make. We're a fresh set. Burdened with the responsibility of trying to make wise decisions even though we're fools, isolated in time.

I mean, if you think about it, you only have to

go back a little over a hundred years, and none of the humans who are breathin' today would be here. Not one of them. We're all new souls. And the fact is that the people walkin' this earth in another hundred years will be a completely different set of souls again, no matter how much our minds try to fool us that we'll be here forever. That's how dependent we are on that thing called memory. Or the things we choose to call our memories. The stories we share with our children. Truth is, those are the only things we have to go on. Whispers from souls gone by. Until eventually, our whispers will be the whispers of souls gone by. Reaching souls that we'll never get to meet. That's how powerful our stories are. And the decisions we make today.

JUST ME

They say that if you don't wash your hair for a certain amount of time, it ends up cleaning itself. I wish it could be that way with feelings. That you could let them fester, deep in the back of your head, until one day you wake up and you've kind of sorted them all out. All neat and tidy and knowing their place. Only you can't do that with feelings. Every so often, you've got to drag them to the front of your mind. Try and deal with them. Head on. Or else you get into the mess I was in recently. Lying in bed, with no idea which direction you should go next.

I was on my way to pick Gwen up when I saw it. Flapping in the January wind. One lonely **Missing Peg** poster still stuck to a lamppost. Missing Peg. Funny how words can flower with new meaning each day. Suppose nothin' stays put in this world. Not even words. Or maybe, especially words.

And that's when I really face up to it. How much I miss her. The excitement of her. The mischief. The mayhem. All that energy she had. I suppose she gave me colour did Peg, sometimes. Gave our family a spark. Only I knew now, she'd been through it herself. She'd suffered and struggled. Much more than I ever had.

♥

Then that night, something a bit weird happened. I was just about to float off to sleep when I heard her voice. As clear as day. As if she was sittin' next to me. Now, everyone else might think I'm bleedin' mental, but I'll always know it was her. A warm yellow glow fillin' my belly. Like the yolk of an egg.

'You're doin' fuckin' marvellous, mun. And don't you forget that.'

I remember opening my eyes in the darkness then. Only there was nothing to see. There was no sleep in me after that. And also, there was something I had to do.

'You alright?' he asked on the other end of the line, his voice full of sleep.

'I'm fine.'

'What's wrong?'

'I don't want to get back together.'

Only he doesn't reply.

'I'm not with that guy. Just in case you were thinkin'. And I want you to have Gwen. Every second weekend. I want you to see this baby too.'

'Okay,' he says, tryin' to figure me out.

'And I expect you to pay your share.'

''Course.'

'Only I want to be on my own. I want you to know that. I wanna be a single Mam.'

He doesn't say anything for a moment. My words reverberating in his head.

'Come over tomorrow if you like,' I say, 'but that's what I want. And that's never gonna change.'

Feeling wide awake, I head to the kitchen to get a glass of milk. Drink down the white liquid in the dark.

'I can't sleep,' I hear her steppin' into the room. Smile at her.

'I've just been on the phone with Daddy,' I say, as she heads over towards me. 'He's comin' over tomorrow.'

'Can I have milk?'

I open the fridge door and pour some cold milk into a purple plastic beaker.

'How's about Mami and you speak Welsh together from now on?'

'Olreit,' she says, downing the milk. Just like Peg used to.

'A Dadi siarad Saesneg gyda ti.'

'Oce. Can I have a biscuit?'

'Cymraeg?'

'Gaf i ca'l bisgit?'

'Oce. Un. Jyst am treat,' a dw i'n trio fy gorau i feddwl yn Gymraeg am munud. Wrth estyn am y biscuit tin. Am practis. Ac am y dyfodol fi eisiau gweld pan bydd fi ddim yma dim mwy. The memory within me. Y stori. It has to start today.

I won't wait for no one else no more.